AN EAGLE BLESSED OUR HOME

Alvin Blackdeer

1926-1988

This book is dedicated to our daughter, Bambi.

May she always be proud of her Indian heritage

AN EAGLE BLESSED
OUR HOME

Published by Skandisk, Inc. 1994
Skandisk, Inc.
7616 Lyndale Avenue South
Minneapolis, Minnesota 55423

ISBN 0-9615394-5-3

Cover and book design
Koechel Peterson & Associates, Minneapolis, Minnesota.

Printed in the United States of America

Skandisk, Inc., publishes *The Tomten*, a catalog which offers exemplary
children's literature, immigrant books, Scandinavian literature, music and gifts.

For more information write to The Tomten,
7616 Lyndale Avenue South,
Minneapolis, Minnesota 55423

AN EAGLE
BLESSED
OUR HOME

Muriel J. Blackdeer

SKANDISK, INC.
Minneapolis, Minnesota

ACKNOWLEDGMENTS

Many of these stories are about the life of my husband, Alvin Blackdeer, as he remembered and retold them to me. I have relied solely on Alvin's reminiscences (and some from other local people) as he did when his father and mother handed down their knowledge from other generations by word of mouth.

Special thanks go to our friends who told me of the days when the land where we lived on Brice Prairie (La Crosse County, Wisconsin), once known as the Old Indian Camp, was a popular hunting and fishing area. Those who shared their memories of a colorful era include Alton Lee, Leo Stuhr, Robinson Johnson, Forrest Bonsack, Bill Koch, Floyd and Sarah White Eagle, Sherman Sieger, and Carl Price.

Special acknowledgments to: Shelley Goldbloom for encouraging me to continue writing this book; to Kate Carter Frederick for her friendship, patience and thoroughness in editing my book (she took a diamond in the rough and polished it into a jewel so precious to me); and to Alvin's relatives, especially my brother-in-law, George Blackdeer, and my nephew and his wife, Richard and Rita Blackdeer, for helping me appreciate the Winnebago way of life.

The people, places and events described within the covers of this book are not to be construed as historical documentary. Many of the people I interviewed told different versions of the same story. It is my wish that through these words Alvin and others who lived in this area will not be forgotten. By knowing and learning things from the past, we should appreciate our present and improve our future.

Muriel J. Blackdeer, January 1991

PREFACE

Alvin and I lived all our married life in a large ranch home on Brice Prairie, near Onalaska, Wisconsin. There were big trees and open spaces that we kept trimmed for our yard. Part of this area was the cemetery used by the residents of the Old Indian Camp located on this property so many years ago. From my windows I could look across the Black River, Lake Onalaska and the Mississippi River and see the hills of Minnesota. We thought we had the most beautiful spot on Brice Prairie. It was from this home I learned to appreciate nature. Alvin and I led active lives in the community but we found lots of time to spend with our family and appreciate our surroundings.

For us, the best time of the year on Brice Prairie was when winter turned to spring: the days of melting snow and ice breaking up on the Black River and Lake Onalaska.

The island closest to our property was slowly being washed away by the river's strong currents. Where once there were five large trees, only two remained and they were bare. This island was so special because every spring, when the ice went out, the bald eagles appeared. For several weeks they roosted in the upper branches of these trees and were easily visible. We have seen as many as 15 eagles at one time—some young, others with white heads that identified them as being at least three years old.

Alvin often spoke of how the eagle was held in high esteem by the Indians. If it was sighted during a feast or event, it was a good omen. It was the Indian's link to heaven. If one thought good thoughts, they soared as high as the eagles fly. The government of the United States even chose this sacred Indian symbol to fly above the flag of our country. It is the only symbol that is allowed to do so.

One day as I was returning home, I spotted an eagle soaring high over our home. It circled over and over directly above the house and as it continued, I called to Alvin and our daughter, Bambi, to witness this beautiful phenomenon. The eagle swooped and glided so gracefully. It seemed to be performing a ritual dance in the air just for us. Alvin looked at this stunning sight and said in a quiet voice, "The eagle is blessing our home." So it was I learned of yet another Indian legend. We have seen the eagle bless our home many times since then.

My eyes beheld an eagle fly
It soared to heights high in the sky
Majestically it glided by
This bird was truly king of the sky.

My eyes beheld a splendid sight
More eagles appeared to my delight
They lit on the stump and they lit on the isle
They lingered for me just a little while.

I watched them dip for fish nearby
I watched them fly throughout the sky
I'll carry this sight 'til the day I die
I'm glad that I've watched an eagle fly.

PART ONE

THE
OLD
INDIAN
CAMP

INTRODUCTION

W hen my husband, Alvin Blackdeer, was eight years old, he dreamed that someday he would build the biggest house on Brice Prairie. His dream was fulfilled when, in 1959, he built our ranch-style house on the same land where his ancestors had camped for more than a century. This beloved land, commonly called the Old Indian Camp, has been known by many other names including Twin Oaks, Swan's Place, White Oak Springs and Oak Springs. Until 1990, an old tree on County Trunk Highway ZB in Onalaska (formerly know as Swan Road) bore a sign that read "Alvin Blackdeer's Old Camp."

The following stories reflect an era during the early 1900's when Wisconsin Winnebago Indians gathered to camp here. The area had long been a favorite hunting, trapping and fishing spot for many people of the tribe. The Black River and its streams held plenty of fish, muskrat and beaver for food, hides and trading. High prairie grasses and large oak trees offered shelter, not only for the people but for an array of birds, raccoons and squirrels. The maple trees were prized for their sap to make syrup. Thick stands of black ash trees grew in swamps and provided material for the women to make baskets and the men to build canoes. There were springs of fresh water for drinking and laundering clothes. It was considered a fine place to keep horses because they could graze and have plenty of water. Campsites and gardens were laid out on the ample, open spaces.

Several longtime residents of Onalaska and Brice Prairie have told of seeing as many as eighteen wigwams and tepees at a time at the Old Indian Camp. Some families came to the campsite annually to hunt and fish. Others simply came to visit relatives who camped there and then they moved on. Still other families migrated from place to place for better hunting, trapping and fishing. According to the old-timers who remember the Old Indian Camp, drums resounded through many nights as the Indians danced around their campfires. Leo Stuhr recalled that young white boys frequently crawled as close as possible to the camp so they could watch the dancers and drummers. It was scary, Leo said, but so exciting that the boys returned again and again.

In 1865, a band of the Winnebagos was forced by the federal government to move from their cherished hunting and fishing grounds in southern Wisconsin to a reservation in Nebraska. The Indians, whose homeland had been ceded to the United States in an 1829 treaty, included those who camped on Brice Prairie.*

Some of the Indians, refusing to move, blended into white communities and stayed in Wisconsin. Eventually many of the displaced people returned to Wisconsin. Among them was a young Winnebago chief named Young Swan (also known as Yank Swan). Hunting and fishing were a way of life for Young Swan. He longed to return to a special place along the river where he had camped with his relatives. He wanted to settle on the land and never be sent away again. Here he would welcome his relatives, friends, anyone—no matter what their race.

Indeed, Young Swan became a pioneer settler at the Old Indian Camp when he returned there in 1881 and began to homestead the land. At the time, the government allowed the Winnebagos to homestead forty-acre parcels, tax free, for twenty years. According to records from the Land and Title Office of La Crosse County, the land passed from H. M. Swarthout to "Young Swan, an Indian and a citizen" in 1903. It is not known if Young Swan paid Mr. Swarthout for the land or if, as was common in those days, the land was given to Young Swan as long as he was willing and able to pay the taxes on it.

When Young Swan came to settle at the Old Indian Camp, he lived in a wigwam. Then he built and lived in a small, wooden house. It was the first permanent building on the land and the only one in the days of the old camp. Many different families occupied this home at one time or another. By 1970, Alvin and I thought the dilapidated shack was too old and potentially dangerous to leave it standing, so we decided to tear it down. We thought it would be an easy job, but it had been sturdily built and constantly reinforced. Finally we used a truck to ram it and pull it down.

Today there are a few remaining landmarks to remind us of the old days. Shortly after the shack was destroyed, Floyd and Sarah White Eagle came to see their old home and were disappointed to see it was gone. As we walked around the property, Sarah pointed lovingly to places near trees and bushes where she had given birth to her children. A large,

---

*"Historical Backgrounds of the Winnebago People," prepared by Nancy Oestreich Lurie and Helen Miner Miller for the Winnebago Business Committee, 1964, pp. 1-2.

clear from all incumbrances whatever_____

and that the above bargained premises, in the quiet and peaceable possession of the said part _y_ of the second part _his_ _____ heirs and assigns, against all and every person or persons lawfully claiming the whole or any part thereof _he_____will forever WARRANT AND DEFEND.

In Witness Whereof. The said part _y_ of the first part ha _s_ hereunto set _his_ hands and seal the day and year first above written.

Signed, sealed and delivered in the presence of

Eugene Johnson

Abner Maynard

Young   Swan   (SEAL)

his thumb mark

_____ (SEAL)

_____ (SEAL)

_____ (SEAL)

State of Wisconsin

La Crosse _____ COUNTY, } ss.

February _____, A. D. 19 _16_, the above named _Young Swan "an Indian citizen"_

Personally came before me this _twenty first_ day of

to me known to be the person who executed the foregoing instrument and acknowledged the same.

D. E. Smith

Notary Public,

La Crosse County,

Wisconsin. _____, A. D. 19____

My Commission expires_____

(To be filled in if signed by a Notary Public)

My Commission Expires
April 6, 1919.

Young Swan's thumbprint on the deed to the Old Indian Camp

old maple tree on the property still holds a rusted pulley, now high in its branches. The Indians repaired their cars under this tree and used the pulley to hoist parts. On May 15, 1987, the Indian cemetery located on our property was given a Heritage Award by the Preservation Alliance of La Crosse in order to protect it as a historical site.

The first permanent structure built on the Old Indian Camp

CHAPTER ONE

LEO STUHR

In 1970, Alvin and I invited Leo Stuhr to our home on Brice Prairie to record all he could remember of the property, the Old Indian Camp and the people who lived and died there. Leo, at age seventy-four, explained why our place had been called White Oak Springs. His memories came alive as he told us stories of the years 1909 to 1911, when he lived a quarter of a mile from the Old Indian Camp. He spent more time here than he did at home. I'll never forget the look of content-ment that came over him as he finished his stories. Leo sat quietly, looking out the window, trying to find familiar landmarks of his youth. The man-made Lake Onalaska had swallowed up the bottom lands he cherished so much. Although Leo was an Onalaska policeman, Alvin remembered him best as the bus driver who drove him to La Crosse when he left for the Great Lakes Naval Training Station.

Leo Stuhr

"My brother, Leonard, and me were the only two white men who knew where the White Oak Springs were. They used to be by a large white oak tree down by the bay, but they're all dried up now and the tree is gone.

"Yank Swan (his real name was Young Swan) owned all this and eight acres across the river and down in the bottoms. There were twelve to eighteen tents right around where this house now stands and one wooden shack—the only permanent building. Some of the Indians who lived here were the Standwaters. I went to school with Nellie. She got TB [tuberculosis] and died when she was fifteen years old. She's buried out here. I went to school with Nellie and Walt Standwater, Jim and George Swan. Jim was about my age. The school was where the Oak Grove School is now. It was a white building that is now in Midway. There was also a Methodist church, too, that was also moved to Midway.

"Anyway, then there was Swan, Otters, Snakes, Charlie Waukon, Russell White Eagle. There was a girl named Dixie; she was a beautiful girl. I think I lived with the Indians more than at home. I was always down here.

"There were lots of ceremonies that took place on this land. I'd hear the drumming at the powwow. I only lived down the road a quarter of a mile so I knew when it was starting. When the sun went down, the drums started. Boom, boom, boom and we'd all run to the powwow. When we got down here, it was scary because they were all decked out in feathers. But we knew them. They'd dance around the drum where the guys would be sitting. We'd even dance around with them. There would be five or six big powwows during the summer. They once tried to get me in to pound the drum. I was only ten or eleven at the time. I got in there with them but I guess I didn't keep very good time because they threw me out!

"Across the river—this, right next to the shore is the Black River you know, is where Swan lived—it was all timber, thick timber. There was eight acres of bottom land. He lived over there in that house the last few years. At that time, anyone who didn't know the country and got out in there hunting, they'd get lost. You just wouldn't know where you were at. Of course I did the same thing myself but I was always

15

lucky to find my way out again. We used to have to go out and get guys—me and my father—at night, especially during duck season. After dark, my dad would go out to the barn, check the stock, come back and say, 'Get your boots on, boy. There's somebody lost in the woods.' We'd take our dog and a shotgun and always a lantern! We'd go down to the river. My dad would shoot, then they would shoot back. My dad would say, 'Do you know where they are?' I'd answer, 'Yes,' and I'd know pretty close where they were. Then we'd go in the bottoms and get them out. The last man we brought out was old Jim Fess. He gave my dad five dollars when he got out!

"It was treacherous bottoms, all right. There were lakes and there were streams in there. You just couldn't move. You'd wander around until everything looked alike to you. I got in there one time hunting up the slashes and my dad said, 'Don't you ever go in them slashes! You'll get lost!' Well, there was a big elm tree, higher than all the rest of the trees. So I got smart, took my hatchet and blazed that tree. I marked the direction I was supposed to start back out to go home and I started off. Then I looked for that tree and I walked and walked and walked. Pretty soon I looked again to find that high tree. I thought to myself, *Is there more than one big tree here*? I kept looking for the tree with the slash I had cut. I tried it three times but every time I tried, I'd always go to the right and I'd always come back to that other tree. Finally I thought I'd fooled myself, so I started in another direction and luck had it I did come out of the bottoms, but way up by another house. I had a long walk back here where I started from. I found out you could get lost all right. I was always told you always go to the right when you get lost.

"One day I met Swan in the bottoms and I said, 'Swan, how you tell where north is?' Swan said, 'Go like this,' licking his finger and holding it above his head. 'Wind show you.' Then he asked me how I could tell. 'I go by the moss on the tree 'cause it grows on the north side,' I said. Swan looked at me and said, 'Huh. Come with me, I'll show you something.' He took me over and showed me a birch tree that had moss all the way around it. 'Your way no good,' he grinned at me.

"Another time, I met him when I was out hunting. He never could say 'Leo,' so he said 'Louie.' I heard somebody holler 'Louie' so I stopped and looked all around. Couldn't see anybody so I started out again. 'Louie,' I heard again. 'Where are you?' I asked. 'Me over here,' Swan called. I went over where I heard the sound and said, 'What's the matter?' He said, 'Me gottum skunks in log and can't get 'em out.' So I said to Swan, 'You cut me a long pole and I'll get them out for you.'

"Swan got a long branch and I twisted it in the log. I could feel the skunks. They started to give a little bit and we finally got 'em going. Swan sat on the other end of the log with a stick, so when the skunk stuck his head out, bang! He'd hit it on the head and throw it to the side. I pushed seven skunks out of that log and Swan sat there and killed every one of them. You could walk on the air! So I said, 'Smells pretty bad, Swan.' 'Yah,' he said, 'but it good for you. You never catch cold!'

"Yah, we'd come down there, us kids, wanting to use one of Swan's boats, see, but he put one back on us. 'If you want to use my boat, you ask me in Indian,' he said. Well, I got so I could, and I could understand it. But I've been away from it for so many years, I've forgot it all.

"Oh, the Indians. There were some bad ones around here, too. They got pretty wild. They'd get a little firewater. Used to go to town in the fall with furs. Well, my folks never used to lock their house. Around eight or nine o'clock, the door opened and a couple of Indians walked right in. Whiskey bottle was getting kinda short, so they poured water out of the tea kettle into their half-empty whiskey bottle and just go home.

"The women used to walk up to my brother's to use their sewing machine to make dresses. They wore big 'Mother Hubbard' dresses that they could sew up in half an hour on a machine.

"When we butchered, Swan always wanted the hog's head, so we'd give it to him. The Indians were poor, but the white people were just as poor. When the Indians would run out of food, they'd ask for a chicken. We'd always share with them.

"Rick and Cross Mather shot a deer and wanted to get the hide tanned. They came to me and wanted to know where they could get it done, so I told 'em to take it down to Swan's. Nobody lived around

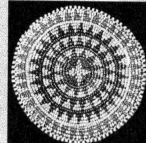

Young "Yank" Swan

there, so I took them down to Swan's as it was dark and he lived across the river. We took a boat, the three of us and the hides, and went across the river. There was ice floating in the water. We walked over there, to Swan's place, and knocked on the door. He'd just holler to come in. We walked in and Swan looked at me and said, 'Louie, how'd you get over here?' 'Come in a boat,' I answered. 'The three of you in one boat?' he questioned. 'Yah,' I said. 'No good,' he scolded, shaking his head. 'Ice on river.'

"We sat and talked about a half hour and he found out they wanted the hair taken off and the hide tanned. When we were ready to go back, Swan said, 'You take one, I'll take one.' We started back across the river and the ice, by God, was the worst I've ever seen. It's a wonder we didn't tip over on the way back. We made it! On the way over, we never even hit a piece of ice. That's how fast the river could become dangerous.

"Swan was a good old Indian. He never could wear shoes. Always had to wear moccasins. He had two heels on each foot, side by side. The back of his foot was real wide. You could always tell when he had walked on the trail by looking at the tracks. No one had footprints like his. Yes, those were good old days, but they are gone.

"This Nellie White Eagle I talked about used to have a sister, Kate, who I used to get letters from. She had the best handwriting I ever saw. She was well educated.

"I used to write Lorraine Swan Winneshiek 'cause I wanted to buy this piece of land here. She wrote back that this land belonged to Indians for so long, she'd only sell it to a Winnebago. Before I knew it, a Winnebago Indian had bought it and it was Alvin! I used to play ball with Alvin's dad when I was only nine years old. Charlie [Alvin's father] was a little older.

"I remember there used to be as many as eighteen families camping here, beside Swan's wooden house, all at one time. That's all the room there was. In the spring or summertime, the shelters would all come down, except the wooden house, and they'd all move up to Black River Falls to pick blueberries and cranberries. Then in the fall, just before the freeze-up, unbeknownst to anyone, here comes a bunch of

Indians. Teams of horses. Four, five, six teams and wagons. They'd come back and set up camp again and stay all winter. This was their home.

"Swan's mother was so old. I used to ask Swan about her and he told me he didn't know how old she really was. She was so old she was carried out into the sunshine on a red blanket and they'd carry her back in at night. Swan's half-brother came up from Nebraska—his name was Donald White—and I asked him. He was trying to figure it out, and said as near as he could figure, she must be one-hundred-eight years old. She died shortly after that. She's buried out there in the cemetery."

Later, Alvin, Leo and I walked outside to the area we knew to be the cemetery:

"Yes, here's the big boulder I remember and this is the tree we used to lean our shovels and picks on when we dug some of the graves." Leo walked around, pointing out sunken areas on the land. "See these places? These are some of the graves you were asking about. They never had markers, but I remember when they had the spirit boxes on them."

CHAPTER TWO

ALTON LEE

I first met Alton Lee down on our boat landing. He was with his son, Bobby Lee, our mail carrier. They both were such friendly, fun-loving men. Together they used to hunt and fish. One day Bobby told me his dad used to know Young Swan. This was the beginning of listening to one of the best storytellers I've ever heard. Alton Lee could tell one story after another and when he quit, you wanted to hear more. These stories were recorded when Alton came to our home in 1983. He was such a good friend of Young Swan's, yet he referred to him as Mr. Swan. It was because of this friendship that Young Swan gave Alton his Indian name, Young Lee.

"The ponies ran loose through the whole woods. There was a fence on the south side that ran down to Broken Gun, but the fence was that way so they wouldn't go to French Island. Here they'd come back on the same path and go out every day in the summer and fall. They were real pretty. Beautiful spotted ponies.

"Coming up the hill there was a gate across the path so ponies wouldn't run loose around Brice Prairie up to Lytles. Mr. Swan or one of his wives would cut up and tie strips of cloth on the barbed wire.

Alton Lee

When we'd come in the morning with headlights on the car, we'd see them deals on the wire and he [Frank Pooler] would stop the car and I'd get out and open the gate so he could drive through, park the car right out here and I'd go shut it. Yank Swan, or Young Swan was his real name, would come out and the first thing he'd look at was the gate. 'Did you shuttim gate?' Mr. Swan would ask. Our answer was always the same, *of course* we had.

"Mr. Swan knew Mr. Frank Pooler. He was a great friend of Indians, like Powell in La Crosse. We always carried a gallon of moonshine because it was Prohibition days. We'd tell Mr. Swan, 'Get a cup and we'll give you some of this.' Next day or so we'd go hunting. Same thing. 'Did you shuttim gate?' He knew the answer but it was an excuse to get more moonshine.

"George Otter had a camp out on Broken Gun and we stayed in our camp further down. We'd come to trap muskrats in the spring of the year and George was trapping turtles on open Broken Gun. When Indians trapped turtles under the ice, they'd look for where the bubbles came up and they'd chop a hole, put their turtle hook down and pick 'em up and kill 'em. They were twelve to fifteen pounds. That's how the Indians made their living, outside of what else they did.

"One Valentine's Day, it was plenty cold and the ground was frozen real hard. We figured it out that Otter had put his sack full of big, heavy turtles over his shoulder and must have been trying to carry 'em to his wife here at this place where he could put them underground with leaves. Well, one of the turtles got his foot out of the wet gunnysack. It scratched and scratched and got its claw in Otter's face and tore his eye out. He bled to death. No one was around to help, so he died all alone.

"We had to bring him in. The Indians asked us to help them bury him. So we chopped and chopped and shoveled and chopped some more. We finally got down in the ground, but it took an awful long time. Instead of going down six feet, it seemed a lot more. The ground was frozen solid. They rolled him in a blanket. I told them I had an awful good friend that was a minister in Onalaska, whose son and I were buddies, who could say a few words. So the minister came out from Onalaska and then they covered him up.

"Otter was buried by the big tree. The rest we buried in a straight line. Three girls died in a flu epidemic during World War I. The son of Swan was killed in an accident and one of his wives died. These are the only ones I remember that were buried here. They had wooden boxes over them, no tombstones. They were called spirit houses and would deteriorate over a period of time. All are buried in a line facing the sun. There were six I knew of and others were also buried. George Otter was buried in 1927 because we built Hoofenpoof, our cabin, in 1926 and it was the next year.

"Down here, Swans had that little house they lived in. Over the hill, down on the landing, that's where the men that lived here did their work. John Mann, and a younger Indian who married Swan's daughter, made their boats there. Not birch bark canoes. They'd go out when this was all woods and cut down an ash tree. You know how tough they are, like an oak. They'd bring it down here through the water, put it up where they wanted and draw a design on it. They didn't use a pattern, just had it in their head. And they made their canoe. This wasn't birch bark. They'd chop and chop and chop with hatchets and dig it out. Then they'd chisel it out with tools they had. Then they'd start a fire and put the coals from the fire in it and that would burn down into the canoe or dugout. The next day, they'd start digging it out again. It'd come out real easy. They'd throw that out to one side. It didn't take them too long.

"They were heavy, green lumber—green logs. Nothing tippier. But we were smart, you know. The river was twelve- to sixteen-foot wide with a bank on the other side. John Mann said, or maybe it was Swan, or both of them said, 'Friend. Dugout. Young Lee.' He pointed to the dugout, so I got in and paddled across. It was tippier than all hell, you know, but I went across and got out. Turned it around by hand, came back and made it back in. There were some other fellas from Onalaska. They were going to do it. Three of them got in (I did it alone), and they got right in the middle and tipped over. I had to wade out and get them. They couldn't get out 'cause they were all tangled up. The boat was on top of them. It was still green and it didn't float good.

"But, the Indians knew how to make them! They used to sell them to museums more than anyplace else. While they were doing this, making boats out of ash, the women would sit and put the ash strips in their mouths, spit out the bark and before you knew it, they had made the most beautiful baskets you ever saw! Out of the scraps from the boat! They put the strips in their mouth to make them soft so they could bend them more easily.

"I've got another good story about Swan. Right down the road, there was one house, way down at the end. That was George Freeman and his missus. Swan, who was a good friend of the Freemans, was to go to town for groceries with ponies and a wagon. Coming home here, he came around the corner with his wagon and saw Mrs. Freeman, who was outside hanging up clothes. Swan said, 'I got the groceries but I forgot something. Wonder if you can help me?' Mrs. Freeman said, 'Well, Mr. Swan, maybe I can. What is it?' 'Some eggs,' Swan requested. 'How many do you want?' she inquired. 'I want two dozen,' he said. She looked at him and asked, 'Do you want to buy them?' 'You fry 'em,' he answered. So she made a whole plateful and he ate them all!

"Yank Swan, or Young Swan, and his family were the only Indians living around here from La Crosse to Trempealeau. There was no one else allowed right here. This was about 1910. You know, he was the chief of the Winnebagos in this area. He came up here from Nebraska.

"This is a true story. Swan hunted, fished and trapped right here all the time. This was at the turn of the century, around 1910. Gun laws changed. Eddie Gautsch was the game warden from La Crosse County. Every once in a while, in the spring of the year, the farmers living around here would report someone shooting ducks up at Lytles and down at Hammond Shoot. So Eddie Gautsch said he'd look into what was going on and report it.

"He went with his boat and found Young Swan trapping muskrat, which was illegal. So he says, 'Swan, I hear a lot of shooting around here. That isn't you, is it?' 'Why?' Swan asked. 'Because laws have changed and you can't hunt ducks in the spring of the year anymore,' he said. 'They closed that. You can hunt after spring, after they've had their young.' Swan said, 'Ain't me. I ain't shoot no ducks.' But the game warden took his paddle and pushed up the straw Swan was sitting on, and there was a shotgun under there. So he said, 'Well, what are you doing with a shotgun in your boat? You know you can't shoot ducks in the spring.' 'I know,' Swan said. 'Maybe, Mr. Gautsch, game warden, maybe I see crow!'

"You had to know Swan to appreciate him. He gave me a beautiful outfit. You'd slip it over your head and wear it like a vest. There were beads all over it, down both the front and the back. Lots of white beads. He gave it to me but I can't find it anymore.

"When the Winnebagos came back from Nebraska, they were given four dollars per month per child. That's why they had so many children. This was a pension from the federal government. Swan had a small garden out here and he hunted a lot.

"I remember one morning in September, Swan and his three wives came out of the house, and when they slammed the door a big flock of blackbirds flew up. Bet it would have covered two or three blocks. Swan said, 'Young Lee, get your gun! Shoot!' So Pooler and I put in light loads that would pepper and we walked out and shot once into the black flock. The blackbirds fell in all directions. The women and children came out and picked up the birds. They picked and they picked. One hundred and thirty-five blackbirds we shot, all lying on the ground.

"'What are you going to do with them?' I asked Swan. He replied, 'Make blackbird pie.' 'That must be an awful job,' I said. We watched them clean the blackbirds. They'd take the blackbird and pull the head off. Then they'd hold it in one hand and put their thumb under the breast bone and snap! There'd be meat about the size of a half-dollar. They'd make blackbird pie and they really knew how to make it. Feathers, legs and the rest were thrown away. I tried to clean 'em but I couldn't. It was fun to watch them, they were so fast. The pie was delicious!

"Other food they ate, well, they used to trap muskrats and dry them on these big racks in the hot sun. They'd dry, dry, dry, and then they'd start a fire and smoke them. These were good! They'd salt some, but that didn't appeal to me 'cause they kept the head and tail, the feet and claws on them. They'd shake them a little and eat them and throw the bones away. They sure liked them. Guess they were good that way too.

"Right across the river here was a dike, twelve to fourteen feet high. It was kept perfect by the Black River Improvement Company, for the logs went down this side and every place there was a break. The dike was higher then, before the lake came in. The logs came from up north. You could walk to Black River Falls without getting your feet wet. In the spring of the year, they were all floated down to La Crosse. When it was high water, they'd come end to end all the way down. They built a shanty, White Oak Springs Shanty it was known as, for their loggers to get spring water to drink instead of river water.

"When the logging days got over with, Young Swan built the most beautiful log cabin you ever saw. John Mann, Fritz Cloud and Swan all worked on it. It was right there on top of the dike. It was beautiful.

"One day, we came and smoke was coming out of the chimney. As we walked by, John Mann opened the door and asked, 'You want to see your good friend Young Swan?' Here they had robes and blankets on the floor and that poor old boy laid there. 'He's very sick,' they told us. 'Stomach trouble.' Well, Frank Pooler said, 'I'll get Dr. Wesson from La Crosse and we'll come up and see if we can help him.' The room was full of smoke, backed up from the fireplace, I suppose.

"We went down and got the doctor and came back with him. They throwed the robes back from Swan and here some Indian doctor had cut, with something sharp like a razor blade, splits all over his stomach. We asked what that was for. 'To let the evil spirits out,' they told us. I can remember this just like it was yesterday, 'cause I stood right there and looked down at my friend, Mr. Swan. Dr. Wesson, a good doctor, listened to his heart and said, 'Well, maybe that's your way of living, but what I'm worried about more than anything is infection getting into those sores.' So he poured iodine or Mercurochrome, a disinfectant, right over the sores. Boy, Swan jumped! The doctor returned in two days and told them Swan wouldn't live. Had something in the stomach. I suppose it was cancer.

"We brought Swan in our car down to the Lutheran Hospital in La Crosse. It wasn't too long 'til Frank Pooler came and got me one night and said, 'We have to go down to the hospital and identify Swan,' which we did.

"Frank Pooler didn't have any money and I was working for fifteen cents at the Onalaska Canning Company and trapping muskrats. But, we all went together—eight or nine of us from Onalaska—Dad, the game warden, lots of others. We got the Methodist minister to say a few words and then took Swan to Pittsville, where they had a good burial. Later, all his old friends went together and bought a tombstone for him. I never knew if it was ever put up but it was bought for him. As you go through the gate, at the Pittsville cemetery, way down on the right-hand side, that's where we buried the Chief of the Winnebagos, my old friend, Young Swan.

"Yes, it was beautiful out here. I'm so sad my grandchildren, even my children, didn't see this place years and years ago with the Black River right here and all the trees before the timber was cut off. Broken Gun, Black Snake, Indian Slough, Taylor Slough, Break-in-the-Way, Gibb Shoot, Hammond Shoot, Wood Shoot. It was so pretty. We never had a camera, so I didn't get pictures. That scenery is just a memory now."

ROBINSON JOHNSON

obbie, a relative and old friend, was always a welcome guest in our home. In 1970, he was visiting area relatives so we asked him to come over and tell us some old stories of our property. Robbie attended the Indian School in Tomah and graduated from Tomah High School in 1927. He had been a member of the last chautauqua in the United States. He was a singer and a dancer, and often told of Indian customs at school assemblies.

At the time of this interview, Robbie was working on a Winnebago-English dictionary. He later took part in a Wisconsin Native American language project at the University of Wisconsin-Milwaukee. Both projects attempted to preserve Indian languages in Wisconsin.

"I recall memories of a visit here with my father about 1922 or '23. That's when old Young Swan and his wife (I don't remember her name, but she was my father's half-sister) lived here. We were here to visit relatives. The thing we noticed was that they had a pet woodchuck. As the old aunt of mine sat there on a rug under the trees, weaving baskets, there lay—seemed to be asleep—a woodchuck. After we'd talked a while, she started talking to this pet woodchuck and started scratching

Robinson Johnson

its back. This animal turned over on its back and she rubbed its stomach. It just lay there motionless. They said this woodchuck would remain with them all summer until late fall and then it would disappear to hibernate. In the spring, like all woodchucks do, it would reappear and remain with them for the whole summer. That's all I remember of our visit here when old Young Swan lived.

"Alvin, you were asking me about Grandfather, Moses Decorah, and what he used to do when he was with the Wild West Show of Buffalo Bill [Cody]. My father used to speak of this. One time, he and Chief Decorah and Jake Decorah—they were blood brothers and they were always together when they were young—they were under the influence of a few drinks. He was talking to my father when I came in the picture and he said, 'Your father, here, used to be a great rider on the horse when we were with this Wild West Show. He was doing fancy riding and rolled around a turn. He ran into a big pole that held up the circus tent and he was badly injured. But it wasn't long until he was back riding the horse again.' They—Jake Decorah, Moses Decorah and Charlie Smoke—were among them too, at one time.

"My father was telling about an incident afterwards. One time they were putting on shows somewhere and they used to eat out. My father went to Carlisle [an Indian college] and could order from the menu. So they asked at the table what my father would order and the rest of them would order. The rest of them would sit there and they'd say to the waiter, 'The same.' So, of course, they got the same as my father did. My father wanted to play a trick on them so he ordered something he knew they wouldn't like too well. Something you'd have to develop a taste for. So he ordered this food and the rest of the men said, 'The same.' When the waiter brought it, they started eating it, after watching my father. They didn't like it so well, but they ate it just the same because they didn't want to feel ashamed of the fact they ordered something they didn't know anything about."

CHAPTER FOUR

FORREST BONSACK

I n 1989, Mr. and Mrs. Forrest Bonsack spent the afternoon with me, reminiscing about their friendship with the people at the Old Indian Camp. Forrest vividly remembered how, in 1934, the bottom lands were cleared before they were flooded to form Pool 7 (now Lake Onalaska). A particularly humorous event he

Forrest and Bernice Bonsack

recalled was when Young Swan moved across the river so he wouldn't be chivareed. In olden days, friends and neighbors gathered wherever newlyweds spent their first night. They pounded on pots and pans with sticks, continuing until the bride and groom brought out treats, usually beer, to the fun lovers so they would leave them alone and go home.

"What I heard and what I know may not be one hundred percent either way. To begin with, Chief Swan homesteaded this land and then he built the house. I imagine he was married at the time. I was quite young then, so I really don't know. He approached A. O. Casberg Lumber Company in Holmen to see if he could get lumber from there to build his little house. He didn't have any money. Nobody did at that time. They said yes, they could stake him for his house. Quite a thing, too. They knew he was honest, so it probably wasn't a great deal of money. In those days you could probably build a house like that for fifty bucks. They gave him the lumber and he put it up. I don't know if he had help, but I'm sure all the people in the Winnebago nation helped him. It was just a simple house. Possibly twenty-by-twenty, with two windows, as I remember it. He agreed to pay it back a little at a time. A dollar now, a dollar then. Which he did. He got it paid for. My dad said he paid for it in full, so he was clear there. Then he lived in it, and as he got a little older, John and Florence Mann and their son, Ralph, lived with him there.

"Then came John Standing Water and his wife and son, Wallace, who was her son from a previous marriage. I imagine he adopted him, I don't know what Indians did in those days. From then, George Whitewater and his family, then Floyd White Eagle (who married Sarah Snake) lived there. Their children went to school up here. So that's as far as I know. John and Florence Mann lived with the chief, but the others came after.

"About where your house is standing now (maybe a little closer to the road) was a great big tepee. Oh, it was immense! It must have been forty feet across and high. This is where the chief and his wife entertained the members of the tribe. They would come here in buggies. By the way, this was all fenced in so they could let their ponies go so they could enjoy visiting or getting advice. I remember going there one time. There was a big oval in the middle lined with rock. They built the fire there. There was a hole in the ceiling for smoke. Buffalo robes covered the floor where they held their council meetings or visits.

"There was a round building (I guess you'd call it a wigwam instead of a tepee), an immense lodge where they all met for their talks. It was made from saplings and covered with tarp as I remember. I was quite young at the time. I was scared to death to go in there because it was dark and smoky. They always sat on the ground, on the buffalo hides.

"My dad, Herman Bonsack, and Chief Swan were great friends. I don't know what the bond was between them. I never asked. But I suspect it was a source of money for the chief. I think my dad gave him money on occasion. Where would he get this money otherwise? A little trapping, a little basket weaving. I'm sure my dad gave him money because he'd come to our house many times. I can still see that spotted-pony team coming up the road. It kind of scared me at first, when I was little, but after a while I got used to it. He would get out of the buggy and his wife would sit in the open buggy. They would talk and I'm sure money changed hands. I don't know what bond there was between them but it must have been Chief Swan's silent power. He was the supreme chief. My dad always said nobody ever questioned his decisions. What he said was law!

"This was around 1920. He was such a quiet man. Didn't look like a chief that you see in pictures. He was a short fellow with slightly bowed legs, with a swarthy complexion. I think he had a toe off. Others said he had wide heels. Whatever it was, it was different, so they could tell where he walked. His footprint was so different.

"The ponies were let loose and they roamed all over the fenced area, over by the graves. Buggies were all over and the people walked all over. It was like an active beehive. They had come to pay homage to the chief, to visit and get direction. I think that was the big thing. 'What do we do now?' was the big question asked of the chief. I remember they had feasts here, but I don't know anything about that.

"Swan was the last of the great Winnebago chiefs in this area because of his power. He and his wife went out to Nebraska every fall. Can you imagine driving that far in an open buggy? They'd camp along the roadside. He'd go out there and was treated like a king, of course. They gave him a new buggy and harness and a team of ponies. That was a big thing in those days.

"I remember one time my dad told me they gave Swan an extra horse that was heavy with foal. She couldn't keep up after a while. My dad asked Swan, 'What did you do?' Swan said, 'We let her go on the road. Left her there. Somebody got a good pony.' They were beautiful ponies, I'll tell you.

"Right over the hill, next to the river, there was a little shack. Swan stabled his horses in there. He had a water tank that was their source of water. I never saw a pump out there. They used the spring water. This place was known as Twin Oaks Spring at one time. There are springs all along the shore but this was a big spring that gurgled into the tank.

"I used to come down and play with Ralph Mann and we'd go down and look over everything. We went out to the cemetery, but we were cautioned not to do anything out there. We had to leave things as they were.

"The chief's wife, during the early spring and summer—the chief, too—would tap trees. There were a lot of soft maples here. It took a lot of them to make their maple syrup. She'd pour the syrup into small containers like a peanut cup. She'd have many, many of those to make her maple sugar. It was so sweet. It was wonderful. She'd give each one of us one for a treat. She used to take them out to Nebraska in the fall because they didn't have maple trees there. Yes, she took a lot of them out there.

"I was with the Indians all my life. Played with them, worked with them, ate with them and hunted with them. It was a routine and I enjoyed it all. I don't know why I never learned the Winnebago language. No incentive to do it. Only learned a few words and I've forgotten them. They were a beautiful people. Calm, quiet, good neighbors. I never heard hollering or ruckus like you do now. It was a quiet time.

"I never knew Jim Swan, but I knew he got killed when a horse threw him while he was racing a motorcycle. Others I do remember were Ralph Mann, who was my best friend. Tom Wallace married Nellie Eagle and they camped over on our land. In fact, the government put up a house for them over there. He helped me quite a bit and she helped my mother. We were good friends. To that union, Mary Edith was born and another little one that died of infantile paralysis when she was little. They were all related to the Swans. We used to go hunting with Wallace every year, including my brother and brother-in-law. Our son used to play with the Indian children, too.

"I'm seventy-eight now and I was about ten or eleven when Ralph Mann and I were such good friends. At that time, the Indians were citizens but they had no rights. But we accepted them as our own. They were no different.

"We used to go to Black River Falls and visit Carrimon's (I believe he was crippled). I'd put a fifty-cent piece in my palm, then we'd shake hands and he'd get the fifty-cent piece. He liked that!

"Nellie Wallace always had fry bread for us when we'd go to Black River for hunting. When my wife and I would go to Black River, Nellie would treat us to blueberries and cranberries.

"I never danced with Tom and Nellie at their powwows. No one had much money during the Depression. Tom used to trap muskrats and Nellie would skin and clean them thoroughly, wash them out good and hang them along the railroad fence by the tail to dry. I can see them yet, dried just as hard as a board. Then she'd pack them in paper boxes after they were thoroughly dried. In the wintertime, when they needed meat, she'd soak a rat or two and that was their food. They did the same with 'coon except she didn't dry them. They ate the meat and sold the hides.

"I never really ate a meal with them, just fry bread, but they'd stop in and eat with us. One time they stopped in. We were having venison, a real delicacy. Nellie would get up and help with the dishes and the men would play cards. We were all in the same boat during the Depression days. I have a three-legged kettle they used to cook in over the fire, years ago. The great big ones were only used for big gatherings.

"These are things I remember and things I was told. My dad could never get over Swan's power. He was a soft-spoken man. Never raised his voice, as I remember. He was just a soft-spoken fellow, but his power was immense. I don't think any king or president had more power than he did.

"My mother was intrigued with Charlie Blackdeer, Alvin's father. He'd light his pipe with a curved flashlight lens that would center all the light in one spot and Charlie would be able to light his pipe that way. It was a regular pipe, not a peace pipe.

"I used to know all the Blackdeers, but lost track of them as they grew older. I knew them all when they were little. Cecelia was a beautiful girl. Too bad she got killed. Then there was Beatrice and all the boys, of course, Donald, Robert, Floyd, Alvin, George, Marlin and Charles. They used to live in a house on the riverbank across the road from where the Blackdeer homestead is now.

"On Arbor Day, we had a picnic at school and then we all came down here to the Indian Camp. Down the road, in the gully, it was overgrown with trees and it was so dark, not much light coming through. We were scared to go through there. Such immense trees that formed an arch over the road.

"Ponies used to graze all over here. People would come, unhitch the ponies from their wagons and let them go out there. They always got them back again. It was a wonderful sight. These people always came to pay homage to their chief. Always. I wish it was today so I could relive some of that again, but it was too much for a little mind to comprehend in those days.

"I don't know what drew my dad and the chief together. They were always visiting. The chief would never go by without stopping. There was a deep friendship and my dad admired his silent power. There is such a thing you know. His power was enormous at the time.

"Swan was married a second time when he lived here. Sherman Sieger used to laugh about it. He was afraid they'd chivaree him, so he moved his wife across the river so no one could reach him! Everyone got chivareed on the prairie!

"Nellie Wallace and Florence Mann used to stop to use our sewing machine to sew their dresses. Nothing fancy. They were always clean and you never saw a spot on those two women. My mother trusted them implicitly. They would help her wash dishes and clean the house. They were good help, but never said much.

"The men did all the talking. They were quiet people, though. If you had an Indian for a friend, you had a friend for life. If you had them for an enemy, they were an enemy for life. They never forgot a thing.

"I was born on the farm. There were the Siegers, Fiers, John Shear's and his brother. Kesslers and Kriesels were later on. They lived across from the store. Andrew Killen lived right off the road.

"Tom Wallace was killed in a car accident. We went to the funeral. I think they stuck a steering wheel in his grave. Jerry, their son, was a pallbearer for a young Blackdeer boy who'd been thrown in the water, got an infection and died.

"Mrs. Bob Schaller [Irene] was a Kriesel girl. She and I are the oldest living residents that were born on Brice Prairie. There are older ones, but we were born here. I'm the oldest, she's next.

"People seemed to come to the Old Indian Camp uninvited, but they were always welcome and came here by droves to visit Chief Swan in the wigwam. I suppose they even slept in the wigwam. They drove from long distances and stayed overnight for a day or two.

"I still have a turtle hook from Tom Wallace. They'd tap through the mud or ice to find them, hook under the shell and drag them out. Half a sack of turtles was about all you'd want to carry. I tell you they were heavy. Tom used to do that, and he'd come back over to our place where we had the car. A sack of turtles like that would weigh a hundred pounds or better!

"When the dams were being built, everyone was astonished at how everything could be cleared and all the trees be cut off in one year. It was so new they didn't know what to think. The contractors set up camp right here. It was all done by hand. No chain saws in those days. The big construction bunk house was located right here on the bank of the Black River. They did all their business, hired and fired, right here. Who gave them permission to be here, I don't know. Anyway, this was the headquarters.

"My gosh, the trees they cut down! They used what they called a jammer that lifted logs thirty feet in the air and piled them high. There were many, many piles a hundred feet long. Then they lit them on fire. Alvin's father was one of the men in charge and did the burning. All the trees were cut in a little over a year. Cut off in '35 and '36. Then the lake was flooded. All the neighbors had teams dragging the logs together so the jammer could pile them. You could take home whatever quantity you wanted at the day's end. This was how they cleared the bottoms. We had two teams out there. Vern Dale had houses skidded across the ice from the islands but I didn't know who helped him.

"When logs used to come down the Black River—that was before my time, but I do remember we had forty acres of wood up on the bottoms—

I'd go up with my dad and see these logs still sitting. They had fallen off the raft and got poked in the mud. My dad, a lot of times, would take a team up there just for that reason and pull the logs out of there. He had a setting of these pine logs—waterlogged—but after they dried out they were pretty good yet. You could see them. They were all up and down the Old Black River, as we called it. Each log had its stamp. Those that my dad took out, we sawed up. I remember we made a hayrack out of some of them. They were about fourteen or sixteen feet long.

"During the logging days, logs were floated down the Black River on big rafts—these were choice logs—down to the Onalaska sawmills. My wife's family used to find these logs, too, near New Amsterdam. The rafts would break up once in a while and they'd scatter all over."

Mrs. Bernice Bonsack joined in the conversation.

"Charlie Winneshiek used to live near New Amsterdam," she said. "That's where I grew up. They were Winnebagos, too. Charlie would come up to the window and look in. If my dad wasn't there, he wouldn't come in. Charlie would always go get our cattle if they were lost in the bottoms. He'd go look for them, and in half a day or so, he'd bring them back to us."

"Yes, my wife's family lived in New Amsterdam," Forrest added. "The Indians lived all over that area there, too. After Young Swan died, though, that ended the great chiefs in this area."

CHAPTER FIVE

CARL PRICE

Carl and Evelyn Price

arl and Evelyn Price visited us in 1970, and together we relived the years when the Indians camped on this property. Carl's remembrances included the old logging days and the stories he had been told.

"About this land, I have to tell you about the time I came down here. It was early spring. I got to talking to Young Swan and I asked him if this was spring. I thought I saw crows flying. He says, 'Sometimes crows fool.' So, in other words, you couldn't depend on the crows flying being a sign of spring.

"He used to come over to our place and get hay for his horses. I don't think they had any money at that time. None of us did. I don't know if they paid for it or not, but they'd go up in the barn and throw down a bunch of hay in the back of their wagon. I don't really know how they fed so many horses. Every Indian had a team of horses and I'd say at least twelve or fifteen tents at one time. They all seemed to have quite a few people in each one. I don't know if each family had a tent or more than one family in each. There was quite a few of them.

"When we first moved here, we'd hear the Indian drums down here when they were having their powwows. It was interesting to listen to, but before moving here the family had never lived in an area where there were Indians. I always liked to read about history and especially about the Indians in the West. I got the opinion from reading books that the Indians had their powwows and drank their firewater and chewed their roots [peyote]. In the books it said they'd get pretty wild and might scalp 'most anybody, so I never dared come down to see what was going on. In fact, I was quite scared.

"Now those tents they lived in, they must have gone out in the bottoms to cut those long willow poles. The tents were sort of round and these poles were bent. I imagine it was canvas stretched over the top [wigwam]. I don't know how much land they had or where the horses were because people and tents covered the land.

"On Sundays, that was the only day I had free, I used to go hunting out there (in the bottom land) and I remember the experience very well. We were invited down to my folks in Onalaska for dinner and I went out duck hunting just before we were going to go. After I came back to the same tree for the third time, I realized I was lost. The stuff about moss growing on the north side of the tree, I didn't take to that. I read once that if you would sight along some trees, you go in a straight line. That's what I did. I finally came out on the river way down south of here and had to come up the levee and cross. As it happened, we were late for dinner and my wife was fit to be tied. She thought I'd drowned or something. The bottoms was treacherous and I wouldn't go out in there at night for several hundred dollars 'cause I'd never get out!

"They used to tell me to listen for the whistle of a train and you could know where to go. But you hear the Milwaukee whistle in a certain kind of weather and it sounds just as close as the Burlington. You couldn't tell.

"At Lytles there, I was told there was a hotel. There was this enormous-big house. At the time, they'd float logs. Also used to run barges up and down there on the Black River at Lytles. It was before I moved here, but I was told about the hotel.

"I remarked to Martin Stuhr about the amount of these logs that were lost, left on the shore of the river. How could it pay to float these logs down, because there were so many left along here. I hauled a lot of them home one year.

"We owned sixty-five acres and that's what they used to call Hammond Shoot; that was through our woodland. Do you remember when they put the dam in up here? They pulled all the logs out and piled them on the bank. They got in an argument about who owned those logs. In the meantime, the high water came up and it took them down into my woodland. We hauled them back up to Lytles where there was a sawmill and sawed them into lumber.

"I asked Stuhr how they could make money when they lost so many logs. He told me they didn't lose one in ten thousand. So you can get an idea of the amount of logs that were floated down the river. The logs were cut way up north, at the beginning of the Black River.

"I was told that each log, like cattle, had a brand on it. When these logs come down they had to have those pens to store each man's logs according to his mark. Everybody's logs were coming down. Then they separated them and each man's went to his sawmill. When the ice went out, they had the drive. I don't know just what other rivers go into the Black River, but there are many others that run into it."

CHAPTER SIX

OUR FRIEND, BILL KOCH

" **A** true friend of the Indians!" "The best historian La Crosse ever had!" These were expressions Alvin used when he first introduced me to the man he respected so much: Bill Koch. Here was someone who had forgotten more Indian history than I would ever learn.

In the early 1950's, Bill Koch took up the cause of preserving Indian Hill, a landmark on La Crosse's north side, as a park. The La Crosse Chamber of Commerce and some developers opposed the idea of a park because they thought it was an ideal spot on which to build a rest home.

Bill asked Alvin to help him with the preservation project. Bill and Alvin spoke at public gatherings, veterans meetings and schools in order to drum up support for preserving Indian Hill. Their purpose was not only to establish a park but to preserve the Indian connection by naming the park Red Cloud. They sought to honor the memory of Mitchell Red Cloud, a hero to the Winnebago tribe, who received the Congressional Medal of Honor after he gave his life to save his comrades during the Korean War. During their speeches, Alvin gave a presentation about Indians and Bill showed many of the Indian artifacts he had collected over the years, in order to stress the importance of preserving Indian history in the La Crosse area. After much effort, Red Cloud Park was dedicated in 1957 with a big parade and an Indian powwow.

Bill and Alvin also worked together to help save the old La Crosse County Courthouse. When they lost that battle in 1965, Alvin purchased seven truckloads of rock from the demolished courthouse. He used this rock for making additions to our home: a patio, outdoor fireplace, steps to a boat landing and an indoor fireplace. Bill made canes, candlesticks and letter openers from wood that he gathered in the old courtyard. He inserted square-head nails and other salvaged materials from the courthouse into these articles and gave them as gifts to his many friends and various dignitaries.

Still another cause shared by the two of them was the naming of the big Indian statue that was created by Anthony D. Zimmerhakl and erected at La Crosse's Riverside Park in 1961. Alvin and Bill were opposed to the Chamber of Commerce's tourism committee's preference to name the statue "Hiawatha." Instead, they thought it should be named after a local chief such as Decorah or Winneshiek. As it turned out, the statue was called "The Big Indian."

Bill and Alvin's friendship lasted more than twenty years. Together, they participated in many Boy Scout events that took them to various towns surrounding La Crosse, including Rochester and Winona, Minnesota. One of Bill's last projects to help Indians was when he led a fund-raising drive for Indians who lost their homes after a devastating flood in Rapid City, South Dakota.

October 27, 1971, was proclaimed "Bill Koch Day" by La Crosse Mayor Peter Gilbertson. A banquet was held at the New Villa Supper Club honoring the ninetieth birthday of this historian. Bill received honors from his pastor, Rev. Edwin Sheppard, Robert Funke of the La Crosse Historical Society, Willard Hanson of the La Crosse Public School System, Howard Fredericks of the University of Wisconsin History Department and Gus Boerner, a former mayor. Chief John Winneshiek and his wife, Lorraine, were guests who represented the Winnebago Indians. Bambi Blackdeer was only four at the time, but she presented Bill with an Indian basket that overflowed with greeting cards from hundreds of friends.

Bill Koch and Alvin Blackdeer examining an Indian cradle

Alvin sang and played his drum while Bambi made an impressive entrance, wearing her new, white buckskin dress, dancing the "Swan Dance." The fringes on her outfit flowed with the beat of the drum as her arms swept up and down like a swan's wings. Bill Koch had often referred to her as an Indian princess.

I was called upon to present Bill with an album made of deerskin and filled with memories. There were pictures of Al and Bill at events. It also included photos of Tom Thunder. There were letters from the offices of various veterans organizations, Rev. Mitchell Whiterabbit and the St. Paul American Indian Center, plus Murray Whiterabbit and the Ashland Bureau of Indian Affairs. The album also contained more than seventy signatures of Indians from Wisconsin, Illinois, Nebraska, Texas and Arizona who happily sent their greetings to *Hom po che Ska* (Red Owl, Bill's Winnebago name). One of these greetings came from Tom Thunder's grandson.

John Merasek was the master of ceremonies that evening. The main address of the celebration was given by Roger Tallmadge (Little Eagle), who at that time was a member of the Governor's Committee on Human Rights.

We all left that evening knowing we had honored a man who had lived and worked hard to preserve the history of the area. He was never afraid to speak out when he was for or against a project. Sometimes he won and sometimes he lost, but Bill was respected for bringing out the truth.

CHAPTER SEVEN

BILL KOCH

"When I was a boy, I was raised at 415 Caledonia Street in La Crosse. I used to put in much of my time on Indian Hill. I went with my father when he used to hunt. Yup, I was only six years old when he'd take me to hunt the Indian Hill area. There were only three houses in the area at the time. We'd hunt the area and knew the Indians 'cause we'd been there quite often.

On our return trip we'd always come over the hill, after we'd hunted between the hill and Medary (both sides of the river), and the Indians were always anxious to know what we'd got. They'd fondle our game and talk amongst themselves. We didn't know what they were talking about. Maybe they were cussing us for killing some of their game. I don't know. Anyway, it was very interesting and we had quite a few friends among them.

Alvin Blackdeer
and Bill Koch

"These were peaceable Indians. We never had any trouble with them at all. The only time any would get into trouble was when they'd go to town after selling furs or hides and get too much firewater. They'd get put in the hoosegow overnight and then be sent home.

"There were quite a few people. Weekends we'd travel over to the Indian Hill just to watch the Indians live and see them around their camp. You could smell the Indian camp a block away because of the tanning of the hides. It's an odor that you don't usually smell, not like cologne. To anyone who liked the outdoors, it was something that would get under your skin and you liked it. That's why so many people would go there to watch them. There were lots of people who liked that smell.

"I remember on one occasion there was a group of people who'd walked over there from north La Crosse to visit the Indians. There was one small boy (probably fifteen years old) and he did something the people there, if they'd got hold of him, would have given him a good spanking for. He got hold of an old, dried-up rat. Had him by the tail. He was close enough to one of the tepees that he threw the rat and it happened to hit up in the poles of the tepee and fell down inside. Just about a minute after that happened, out come an Indian with an ax in his hand, and his eyes were blazing fire! That kid turned around and I guess he's running yet!

"Yup, that was about 1890. The Indian finally went back into his tepee. Things kinda cooled off and people started to disperse about that time. They weren't too anxious to stay around much longer after some-one had pulled a trick like that on the Indians, 'cause the people on the north side of La Crosse didn't feel that way towards the Indians. The kids, of course, were full of pranks and they were liable to pull any-thing. You didn't know what they'd pull next.

"The Indians stayed on the hill until the fall of the year when they'd leave and go north along the La Crosse River to Black River to hunt. They'd gather meat and do the trapping, and in May of every spring they'd return to Indian Hill. They'd put up their wigwams and tepees again and then they'd be in business for the summer.

"This was their village and they would trade some of their hides

Chief John Winneshiek and Alvin Blackdeer presenting Bill Koch with the name "Hom Po che ska" (Red Owl) on July 4, 1963

that they brought back. They sold some, of course, to the traders here. John Levi, who died in 1910, was an Indian trader who traded with the Winnebago Indians until he died. He'd buy some of their hides and there were others, too, of course. They kept some of their hides for clothing or whatever they wanted to use them for.

"They'd tan these hides at the foot of the hill, in the water. They'd come in over the east side of what is now Red Cloud Park, just before you get to the railroad tracks. There was a bay at the foot of the hill where they'd spread out their hides in the water. That was the first step of the process that they'd do to tan their hides. Then they'd stake them and mark them so they could identify them. There were boys who used to walk over there and do a lot of frog spearing along the edge of Indian Hill. There were many frogs over there. The boys would go over there in the spring and spear those frogs. The Indians appeared at the edge of the hill and would caution us not to throw spears in their hides 'cause it would make holes in them and they didn't want these hides dam-aged. We never got into any trouble with the Indians on that score at all. This was just how they lived.

"Later on, after I was employed by the Wisconsin Pearl Button Company, I grew up and got married. I later became the superintendent of the button company and it was my job to buy all the raw materials for the company. I found some of the Indians up on Black River digging shells up there and I used to buy their shells. Then I made my acquain-tance with them. It was there I got very well acquainted with Tom Thunder, who was the chief of the group of Indians up at Hunters Bridge on the Black River.

"They had about thirty Indians there digging these shells at what was called Fort Norway. This was the place that housed the lumberjacks and loggers who worked for the sawmill during the sawmill days. It was at this location that they had their camp and I'd buy all their shells.

"I was the only buyer or business who could buy shells from them. We had competition for a lot of these clam shells for buttons. They'd come up here from Muscatine, Iowa, trying to buy shells from the Indians, but the Indians would never sell them the shells. One day, one of the head buyers from Muscatine came down and stopped to talk to the president of the Wisconsin Pearl Button Company. He wanted to know from him what Koch had on the Indians up there that nobody else could buy their shells. He said, 'Well, he knows quite a lot of them and is quite friendly with them. He's known a lot of them since he was a boy, and I guess it'll be hard for anyone else to buy from them.' This fella had gone up there and offered them a dollar more than Koch had been paying them but, as Tom Thunder would say, 'Boss, he pay more, too.' So he couldn't buy them.

"I was always very friendly with Tom and his people. Later on, I became acquainted with Alvin Blackdeer through Rev. Mitchell Whiterabbit and his brother, Murray Whiterabbit. Alvin and I have been together on many crusades. Mainly the creation of Red Cloud Park and a few other crusades we were cooperating together on. We became quite friendly.

"There is one incident I'd like to speak of that impressed me very much. When I was a small boy, fourteen or fifteen years old, this tragedy happened during the winter months in one of the Indians' wigwams on the La Crosse River near Indian Hill. As I said before, the Indians left Indian Hill during the fall of the year to go on their hunting trips up and across the Black River. There were always three or four lodges that would stay behind. They would trap in the bottom land between Grand Crossing and what we then called Lake Park. We didn't call it Myrick Park. In them days, there was a lake behind the park. This was all swamp area and very good hunting and trapping grounds. These few Indian lodges stayed to take in the trapping in this area.

"It was during the cold days of the winter that their wigwam caught afire. There was an old man in it. I'll bet this old man didn't weigh more than about ninety pounds (didn't *seem* to weigh more than that). He was all shriveled up. But he had his son or somebody else there, a big man, and they were all staying together. Well, the wigwam caught afire and in the process of trying to put out the fire, this old man's hand and arms were burned quite severely.

"I happened to be at the Rose Street bridge going down to help my father, who at that time had charge of the switch lamp for the Milwaukee Railroad. I noticed two Indians walking up the street. I could see there was something the matter with the old man. I saw them stop at a brick house on the southeast corner of Island and Rose Streets, right alongside of the North Street viaduct. In those days, it was a wooden bridge.

"Well, the old man walked up the steps of the brick house and rapped at the door. I was curious and watched what was transpiring. What happened was, I seen the door open and there was conversation. They were at the door for a minute, or a minute and a half. Then I see this old man turn around and walk down the steps and when he was partly down the steps, I see him topple over and fall down. He hit his head on the brick wall that was right along the brick steps. Well, the man that was with him, the big man, he walked up and picked him up in his hands, raised him above his head and started to walk in a circle while he was chanting something. I don't know what this was. Evidently, he was trying to bring the old man to. It was only a few minutes later that somebody must have called the police. Anyway, the police arrived and they took him away. I suppose they took him to the station and got a doctor to give him care.

"That always impressed me very much. I never forgot it. I always felt sorry for that old man. I resented the fact that they turned him away at the door and didn't try to do something for him.

"Perhaps I should mention to you, before I forget it, that White Beaver [Dr. Frank Powell] was the official medicine man of the Winnebago Nation as well as the Sioux Nation. He had his home up on Indian Hill and it stood on top of the knoll above the rubber mills. It was a big home and it had a tower or cupola on the top of it. He, at one time, was on a hunting trip up around Black River Falls around 1880 and Chief Winneshiek was ill with fever. He was quite sick and the local medicine man was treating him but didn't seem to do much good. The Indians found White Beaver hunting out in the woods. They knew him, of course, because he was a part-Indian [Seneca] himself. They told White Beaver about the illness of Chief Winneshiek and wanted him to come to the wigwam to see what he could do for him. So White Beaver went to the Winneshiek lodge and examined him and treated him. After he'd been with him for some time, perhaps a couple of weeks, the chief started to improve. He got so he could smoke his pipe again and go out hunting. After the Indians saw Chief Winneshiek was going to recover, they held a big powwow there and officially made White Beaver the Medicine Man of the Winnebago Nation.

"I remember when I was a boy, you'd see the Indians along the curb of White Beaver's office. Where the Yahr Lang Drug Company was [now the Powell Building], there was his office on the second floor. I'd see the Indians ready to go up to see White Beaver to consult him about some ailment they had or maybe just to talk to him. Well, they had to wait for his signal to come up.

Dr. Frank Powell

"I should also mention that White Beaver and Buffalo Bill were very good friends and business partners. Buffalo Bill was an Indian scout during the Wild West days and White Beaver was an army physician and that was where they got acquainted. After they left the army, they used to visit together and got to be very good friends.

"White Beaver had an observation tower on Indian Hill. This tower, as I remember it, was about as high as a three- or four-story building. The dimensions were about twenty foot by twenty foot. It seemed to be square, and was built out of timbers and planks. It had a stairway clear to the top. At the end of each flight of stairs, there was a floor, so anyone climbing up into the tower could go up as high as they wanted to and then look out over the country.

"Now I never did hear why they had the tower there. Evidently it was an observation tower so you could look over the surrounding area. I myself climbed up into that tower many times as a boy, but I noticed in later years that it began to get rather shaky. We'd get up to about the third floor and we'd notice the tower would weave a little. It wasn't solid like it was previously, in the beginning. I think White Beaver noticed it himself and had the thing torn down. That was the end of the observation tower.

"This carved cane I have is carved out of one piece of wood and is supposed to symbolize the Messiah, who the Indians believe will return to the earth during the Ghost Dance days of the Sioux Indians. During that time, there once was a Peyote Indian who had a dream that an Indian Messiah would return to earth and bring with him all the dead warriors that white men had killed. They, together with living Indians, would drive the white men back into the sea where they came from. Now this Indian carved this cane to symbolize the coming Messiah.

"The head of this cane is supposed to be the image of the Messiah. He has two braids coming over his shoulders. In the back, between the braids where the hair separates, is the carved tepee. That's the tepee where the spirit would sleep. The cane itself represents a bow. It's notched at both ends and has an arrow and a peace pipe in back of it. This is all one piece of wood. It's an interesting piece of art that I think quite a bit of.

"Now the Indian people, according to legend, also had a flood like the white men. The legend simply states: Many years after the Messiah created the earth and people, they began to war with each other. They had a lot of trouble, which displeased the Great Spirit. They had a great flood and when it occurred, they all left for the Mound of the Prairie. Well, this Mound of the Prairie, according to the Sioux, was located at Pipestone, Minnesota.

"They tried to dismount there and were drowned by the oncoming water. It seems the higher they climbed up the mountain, the higher the water would rise. Just as the water was about to cover the top of the mound, an eagle was flying over the top of them. An Indian maiden grabbed a leg of that eagle and it carried her over to a nearby cliff that had not become covered with water.

"Here, she gave birth to twins. These twins, according to the legend, repopulated the earth. Now many hundreds of years after this, when the earth was repopulated, the Indians again began to war with each other and fight. So the Great Spirit sent runners to all the tribes of Indians and called them to the Mound of the Prairie. He wanted to talk to them.

Well, they came from all directions and they stood at the bottom of the mound, glaring at each other.

"The Great Spirit appeared at the top of the mound and reprimanded them for being at war. He told them there was plenty of land for all of them and plenty of game and other supplies they could get, so there was no cause for quarrels or wars.

"While he was reprimanding them, he reached down and picked up a piece of red stone and he made a pipe out of that stone. He began to smoke it while he was talking to them. He explained to them that the red stone he had fashioned into a pipe had been the flesh and blood of their ancestors who died there in the great flood centuries ago. He advised them that they should take this stone home with them, fashion pipes the same as he had and smoke them at their gatherings. They were to pray for peace, whether the gathering was with white men or Indians or whatever they were. They should always smoke the peace pipe and be peaceful among each other.

"Now since that time, you will note, the Indians did come from far and wide (and still, today, come) to Pipestone, Minnesota. It is the only place known where this pipestone is available. To secure this stone with which to make the peace pipe, you can go to tribes in the south or far north and you'll find peace pipes made of pipestone that was taken from the mines at Pipestone, Minnesota.*

"I've enjoyed the many hours I've spent with you, Alvin, going to various schools and Boy Scout camps where I'd have all my Indian trophies with me and give the people the history of the trophies I had. I've always been very interested in the Indian and I've always done everything I could for them. The Indians' interest, like Rev. Whiterabbit's and yours, in taking part in both white man and Indian activities is certainly a credit. I think Rev. Whiterabbit has done a marvelous job at the Black River Mission. The speech delivered by his brother, Murray, at the Red Cloud Park dedication was a masterpiece. I don't think Abraham Lincoln ever delivered a speech any greater than the one Mr. Whiterabbit delivered that day.

*See Chapter 25, page 138, for the "official" legend of Pipestone.

"We could go on and on about Indian history and the way the white man has treated the Indian. I've always hoped I'd live long enough to see the white man repay all the Indians for all the resources and land, at least part of it, that they have really taken and stole from the American Indians."

Alvin Blackdeer, Nellie Red Cloud and Bill Koch. Bill presenting the proclamation naming Indian Hill "Red Cloud Park" in honor of Nellie's son, Mitchel Red Cloud. Mitchel was awarded the Congressional Medal of Honor.

CHAPTER EIGHT

THE BIG SQUASH

One of the stories Alvin remembered his mother telling him was about an old Indian woman who saved her squash seeds year to year and always had the largest and best-tasting vegetables at the Old Indian Camp.

One day, the La Crosse County Agricultural Agent (a white man) was driving down the road to the landing near the camp when he spotted this well-kept garden with its bountiful produce. The old woman was checking on her vegetables, so he stopped his car and went over to talk to her.

"Hello there," he said, coming closer to her garden. "My, you have beautiful vegetables. That squash over there is a real prize winner."

"Hmm," she replied and walked away.

He continued on his way to go fishing off the shore of the river. Later he came back and stopped again to talk to the lady.

"Where is that big squash? Did you change your mind? Can I take it to the fair?" He was sincere because he knew she had a blue-ribbon squash.

"Squash for Indian. Not white man. Make soup."

So that was the end of the big squash!

CHAPTER NINE

MOSES

oses Decorah, son of Four Deer Decorah and descendent of Chief One Eye Decorah, was Alvin Blackdeer's grandfather. He was a handsome and impressive man with a six-foot-six-inch frame. Moses was born in 1855 and lived during the time when bands of Indians were still fighting each other. It wasn't uncommon for Indians to kill each other for no reason at all.

He lived near Wyeville with his wife, Kate Whitedeer Decorah. Moses and his family, like many Indians at that time, moved to different areas at different times in order to find means of support. They lived around Wyeville during the cranberry harvest season and in the La Crosse area during the hunting, trapping and fishing season.

One day, Moses made a move that changed the course of his life when he left home to walk to Tomah for supplies. At the time, there was just a rough road that went past the Indian school, located where the Tomah Veterans Administration Medical Center now stands. When Moses never returned from his errand, it was assumed he had been ambushed and killed by renegade Indians.

What really happened was Moses met Buffalo Bill Cody in Tomah.

Moses Decorah, Alvin Blackdeer's grandfather, at age 67

Buffalo Bill offered him a job as interpreter for the Wild West Show. Moses not only spoke Winnebago and English but he was an excellent horseman as well. The show was packing up and getting ready to leave Tomah, so Moses had no time to notify his family of his plans. Two years later, he returned home with stories of his travels throughout the United States and Puerto Rico.

After his return home, Moses continued his friendship with Buffalo Bill. The two were mutual friends of Dr. Frank Powell, who the Indians knew as White Beaver and recognized as a medicine man. Dr. Powell willingly treated the Indians, but there was a lot of prejudice at that time. When Indians sought treatment from White Beaver, they were not allowed to wait with white people in the waiting room. Instead, they had to wait outside, across the street from Dr. Powell's office, until the last patient left. Then Dr. Powell motioned through the window to let them know they could come up to his office.

Alvin's mother, Caroline, was the daughter of Moses and Kate Decorah. One of the stories that she passed on to Alvin was about Dr. Powell. He often contacted Moses, his trusted friend, to run errands for him. Since Moses owned a horse and wagon, he went to various houses to pick up cargo for Dr. Powell. One stormy night, Moses was sent to Barre Mills on what he thought was a rather secretive journey. When a strong wind blew the tarp off the wagon, Moses saw his cargo: a corpse. Moses was a superstitious man and that was the last trip he made to pick up any unknown cargo for his friend! Although those were the days when money was scarce, if you were hired for a job, you never asked questions. In this case though, from then on, Moses did!

Alvin's mother told another story of a time when the family jour-neyed to La Crosse and stayed in a hotel for the first time. This hotel building once housed the Thorpe Financial Company but has since burned down. The family was there because a new drinking fountain was to be dedicated. Moses was invited to take part in the fountain's dedication. Dr. Powell presented the stone fountain as a gift to the city of La Crosse. It had the date "1890" on one side of the base, "Dr. Frank Powell" on another side, "Lob ska ska" (Sioux for "White Beaver") on another side and a white beaver carved on the fourth side. After the

Buffalo Bill Cody as he appeared during the time of his Wild West Shows

Kate and Moses Decorah, when Moses returned from his travels with Buffalo Bill. Note the cowboy hat combined with his Indian clothing.

dedication speeches, Dr. Powell took the first drink from the new fountain. Buffalo Bill took the second drink and he was followed by Moses
Decorah. The fountain originally stood on the corner of Second and Main
Streets. Today, having survived road expansions and traffic accidents, it
has been restored and stands in the lobby of La Crosse's City Hall.

Alvin remembered his grandfather, his Choka, as a very tall, well-
built man with long, gray hair that hung down over his shoulders.
Sometimes Moses wore his hair in braids, but it was never in his face.
Alvin vaguely recalled his Choka standing by a campfire at their home.
He wore overalls but was bare from the waist up except for the blanket
that always covered his shoulders.

During one of the family's feasts, Moses bestowed upon Alvin the
Indian name *Hump he rrue cun e ga*, which meant "Boss of the Day."

After Moses died in the early 1940's, his wife went to live with
Alvin's parents. Kate Whitedeer Decorah is buried in the Indian cemetery on a hillside south of La Crescent, Minnesota, near the home of
her close relative, Virginia Decorah.

Bambi Blackdeer standing by the
White Beaver Fountain

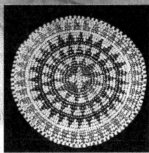

CHAPTER TEN

TOM THUNDER

om Thunder was Chief of the Wisconsin Winnebagos for almost fifty years, during the first half of the twentieth century. He was born in a tepee and lived, as many Winnebagos did, traveling and camping where there was good hunting and fishing. He was once described as "straight as an arrow, lithe and active, being a leader in games of skill and agility." Tom was the son of John Thunder, an Indian medicine man.

Tom Thunder often traveled to Washington, D.C., where he fought for treaty rights and claims on behalf of the Winnebagos. It was said that he was an imposing figure as he walked the capital streets in his beaded costume and feathers.

Tom was recognized by everyone by his huge nose. It was said he had a growth that was removed but that it grew back again. According to a newspaper account, he was like a "new man" when he had his nose "removed," but no one recognized him anymore.

One of Tom's old friends was Bill Koch of La Crosse. Bill told us that Tom had two wives at a time when most men couldn't even afford one. Tom Thunder knew Bill to be an honest man, so every fall he brought

Tom Thunder and his family. A well-known figure in the La Crosse area, Tom died in 1949, at the age of eighty-two.

his most prized possessions, including many beautiful beaded artifacts, and hocked them to Bill. Tom received a money loan from Bill, but he always returned in the spring to reclaim his things and repay the loan. Bill explained that he never let on, but he knew Tom had no safe place to keep his treasures, so he trusted Bill to do it for him.

Tom Thunder died in 1949, at the age of eighty-two.

CHAPTER ELEVEN

A REMINDER OF THE PAST

A large, open space on the Blackdeer property looks like a lawn but it contains an Indian cemetery. During the years of the Old Indian Camp, when Indians died here, they were buried near their campsite. There are approximately eighteen Indians buried at this location. Most of them died of measles or during the flu epidemic around 1918. At the time, the Indians did not always know why their people were dying, so they were afraid to touch the dead because they might also get the disease. When an Indian died, the body was wrapped in a blanket and rolled onto a big piece of canvas, then two long poles were used to carry it to the cemetery. During the measles and flu outbreaks, there were few able-bodied Indians to help with the burials. Local white people came, out of the goodness of their hearts, to help dig the graves. Alton Lee and Leo Stuhr were two of the white men who helped them.

One of the people buried in the Indian cemetery is Jim Swan, Young Swan's son. Sherman Sieger told the story of how Jim Swan died. At the age of twenty-three, Jim was considered the best horseman in the area. When the first motorcycle appeared on the prairie, Jim was challenged to a race. A nearby farmer, who had the fastest horse, offered to let Jim race with this horse. Jim passed the motorcycle, but when they reached the home farm of the horse, Jim turned to see where the motorcycle was just as the horse turned in "his" driveway and threw Jim off balance. He fell off the horse and was badly injured. Jim's battered body was loaded into the back of a farm wagon and brought back to the Indian Camp. He refused a medical doctor, thinking he would be all right, and then died several days later from internal injuries.

Others buried in the Indian cemetery are June White Thunder, Dale White Beaver, Baby St. Cyr (her mother was white, her father Indian), Dale White Eagle and the Greendeer baby (twin of Fredrick Greendeer) who died at birth in 1926.

Leo Stuhr told of a Civil War veteran who was buried there and an Indian who was brought up the Mississippi River from Lansing, Iowa, to be buried with his relatives. Della Standing Water, an Indian maiden, was also buried there.

Three of Yank Swan's young daughters died during the flu epidemic. Alton Lee, Leo Stuhr and Frank Pooler helped bury them in the Indian cemetery. Alton described how they were all buried in the traditional Indian manner: in a straight line facing the sun. George Otter was probably the last person to be buried there in 1927.

Indians did not place markers on their graves. Instead, they laid a wooden box (with both ends open) on top of the grave. These were known as spirit houses. After fifteen to twenty years, the box would deteriorate and disintegrate. Then, the Indians said, the spirit of the deceased would have escaped.

The cemetery was always an inviting area to picnickers and campers because it was just like being in the wilderness. It also had a flat, open space that was just right for a camp or picnic. Years ago in the summertime, the Indians left the Old Indian Camp and went blueberry picking near Black River Falls and Millston. Then they moved on to harvest cranberries around Warrens and Mather. By late summer, they returned to Brice Prairie for hunting and trapping. One year, when the Indians returned, campers had taken the spirit houses from their cemetery and used the wood for campfires.

Preparing for the Ghost Feed at the Old Indian Camp.
Alvin is on the right, his sister Beatrice is standing.
His mother has her hair covered with a scarf, which
was common Indian dress. The other person is a
blind woman who lived with them.

Indians treated death as being part of life. Special meals, such as on Thanksgiving or birthdays, were shared with the cemetery. Small portions of food were taken from each dish and brought to the cemetery with a prayer before others partook of the food. This tradition is continued today.

Another Indian custom connected with the cemetery is for young children.* They go to the cemetery with one of their parents after they have lost their first tooth. They say a prayer and put the baby tooth behind a tree. This custom is part of their growing up.

"Today is a good day to die," was a familiar Indian phrase. There was no fear of death. The occupants of this small cemetery on Brice Prairie led normal lives. Some died very young. Others died old. Some met death through accident. Most met death through disease. May their final resting place remain undisturbed. May they rest in peace.

* When Bambi lost her baby tooth, Alvin told her they were going to place it behind the tree in the cemetery to exchange it for a strong fang of a snake. This would become her permanent tooth.

PART
TWO

ALVIN
BLACKDEER

INTRODUCTION

Alvin Blackdeer was a man of many talents and great ambition. All during his youth, Alvin dreamed of two things: to ride in the head engine of the big, steam-powered trains that he could see as they passed on Brice Prairie and someday wear the shiny badge of a lawman. He achieved both these things. As a full-blooded Wisconsin Winnebago Indian, Alvin lived with one foot in the Indian world and one foot in the white world. One word describes him best: proud. He was proud of his service in the U.S. Navy and his active dedication as a veteran, as well as his thirty-two-year career with the railroad.

Although his railroad friends dubbed him "The Chief," Alvin could never be a real chief because he was a descendant of the female side of the chief's (Chief Decorah's) family.

An active figure in the community, Alvin served as a La Crosse County deputy sheriff for eleven years. He was a constable for the Township of Onalaska and a supervisor on the town board for many years as well.

One of Alvin's biggest assets was his good humor. He was devoted to helping others see the bright side of life. If he believed in a cause, he fought for it. He was kind and sincere. He raised six foster children as well as his own two daughters and six stepchildren, vowing to do his best to see that they could enjoy some of the luxuries he had missed as a child.

Alvin followed his Indian religion and taught me to love and respect all things God had put on this earth. He believed that everything, from each blade of grass to all animals, was placed here for a reason. He never killed an animal unnecessarily. When a snake was sunning on our sidewalk, would Alvin kill it? No! He used a branch to pick it up and toss it into the lake.

When spring came and the animals near our home gave birth, Alvin pointed out these special events. One year a skunk had beautiful twins and so did a woodchuck. On the river, ducks were a familiar sight, as ducklings paddled after their mother in a follow-the-leader fashion and learned how to swim.

Alvin and I led active lives in the community but we found lots of time to spend with our family and appreciated our surroundings.

CHAPTER TWELVE

ALVIN AS A YOUNGSTER

A beautiful Indian maiden, Gladys, was the oldest daughter of Charles and Caroline Blackdeer. In 1928, she lay dying in a darkened room at their home near Wyeville.

"Why do these things happen, Ma?" she inquired of her mother. Like so many Indians at that time, Gladys was dying of an unknown disease.

"I cannot answer you, my dear. Try to sleep," comforted her mother. Deep in her heart, Caroline knew someone had used witchcraft or poison on her beautiful teenage daughter. This was common practice among envious Indians and many were envious of Gladys' beauty.

"Ma, don't stay here after I'm gone," Gladys whispered. "There are too many sad memories here."

"I couldn't bear to leave you and Levi here," the mother replied as she brushed back the hair from her daughter's fevered brow. Levi, her oldest son, had died of spinal meningitis.

"Get Pa to move to Midway. We've always been happy there, Ma. Ma," she moaned, "let me see my little brother again." The family, like many Winnebagos, migrated from the Midway area during the hunting and trapping season to the Wyeville-Warrens area for the cranberry and blueberry season.

Caroline went outdoors and motioned to her youngest son, Alvin. She took the boy by the hand and led him to his dying sister's bedside. Gladys held the boy tight, kissed him on the cheek and said goodbye. Alvin went back outside to play. Shortly afterwards, when the others came out, he knew she was dead.

Soon after Gladys' death, the family followed her wishes and moved to the Midway area. The move proved to be a wise one. Their first home was a wigwam on the shore of the Black River, beneath the bank of the Old Indian Camp on Brice Prairie. Plenty of fish, muskrat and beaver provided a good living. They would never again go hungry.

The Blackdeers' permanent home was built on the bank of the Black River, several miles from the Old Indian Camp. They did not live at the Old Indian Camp because Peyotes had moved into the area and Alvin's mother belonged to the old Medicine Lodge.

Charles (Charlie), Alvin's father, had worked on the railroad in Wyeville and was happy to get work out of Midway on a railroad section crew for the Chicago Northwestern Railroad.

Alvin was born on March 29, 1926, at Valley Junction near Wyeville, with the assistance of a midwife, Mrs. Rachael Littlejohn, his grandmother's youngest sister. He was born with a growth on his neck and wasn't expected to survive. Doctors never suggested removing the growth. Finally, when he was about seven years old, the growth just disappeared.

In 1934, Alvin's eye became infected so he couldn't be in the sunlight. A canvas was placed over the car and he sat in it all day long until dark. He either slept or welcomed anyone who came to sit, talk or play checkers with him.

That year, his brother Donald worked on the Mississippi River dam project. Robert stayed at the Furlong farm where he was employed. Floyd and Alvin stayed home, while the girls and parents went to the Wisconsin Dells for summer jobs.

When their parents were gone, Vern Dale was like a guardian to

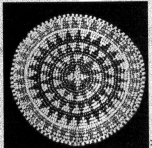

Charlie and Caroline (Decorah) Blackdeer

the youngest Blackdeer children. He stopped in to make sure they had food in case they had forgotten to go to the Van Loon General Merchandise Store for groceries. Their parents had established a charge account agreement with John Van Loon, the store owner. There was only to be nourishing food. No candy!

One day, Alvin developed an unsightly boil on his hand. It was very swollen and painful. He was unable to move his thumb. Vern took one look at it and told him to be ready late that afternoon, when he would take Alvin to the doctor. After Vern left, Floyd said in a scary voice to the already-frightened Alvin, "We better open that with a pin or the doctor is gonna take a big knife and cut you open!" Needless to say, blood and pus squirted out when the boil was pricked open. Then what should they do?

Alvin remembered that his pa always said, "Manure will take out the poison." So they found some manure, put it in a work glove and slid Alvin's hand into it. He kept it there the rest of the day. Luck was with him, for when Vern returned to pick him up, the hand was back to normal. The biggest surprise of all was that no other infection developed. Alvin was grateful the doctor didn't have to use that big knife on him!

Vern Dale and Charlie Blackdeer were as close friends as you could find. One day, they decided to become blood brothers. Charlie took his hunting knife and cut his own wrist, then Vern did the same. They bound their wrists together, letting their blood flow freely into each other's veins, binding their friendship forever.

Vern Dale told Alvin and me that story one day when we visited him at his factory, Outer's Lab. He also told us how he had named Blackdeer Road in honor of his friend. The road is now known as Northshore Drive, but old maps still have the Blackdeer name.

When Lake Onalaska (Pool 7) was formed in 1935, Vern bought the houses on the islands for a dollar apiece and brought them to shore on barges. The Kramer brothers operated the barges and let the Blackdeer boys ride on them.

The old house on the Blackdeer homestead was the old Jake Schaller home that was brought to shore from Schaller's Island (also known as Red Oak Ridge). The Blackdeers wanted a larger home, so

Vern brought the Schaller house over for them. After the lake came in, Vern traded land with Charlie. Vern acquired the lake frontage and the Blackdeers received their homestead site.

Today, George Blackdeer (Charlie's oldest living descendant) lives in a small home on the old homestead property. Charlie's grandson, Richard Blackdeer, and his wife, Rita, live in another home there. Robert LaMere, another grandson of Charlie's, lives in the original house brought across the river.

CHAPTER THIRTEEN

A BIG LITTLE INDIAN BOY

D uring Alvin's grade-school years on Brice Prairie, the Blackdeer children attended school where Metallics factory now stands. Their home was located about one mile north of the school. This was during the Great Depression of the 1930's, when whites and Indians shared the hardships of the times. There was very little money and what there was had to go to feed the family. There were no fancy dinner buckets in those days. All the children used syrup pails to carry their lunch-

Alvin as a boy

es. Butter was not available, so lard was spread on their sandwiches. No one cared about being poor because everyone else who attended school was just as poor.

About 1934, the Indian school at Neillsville did away with its school uniforms. The federal government wanted Indians to forget their identity and start looking, acting and living like white people. Until then, teachers and students at the school had worn these uniforms.

Schoolhouse, circa 1935

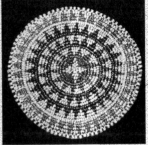

Marlin, George and Alvin

The jackets were olive drab with brass buttons, like old army outfits. They were nice and warm but all looked alike. For a dollar a box, Ben Stucki at the old Indian school would ship a box of uniforms to fit indicated sizes—small, medium or large.

One of these boxes arrived at the Blackdeer home one day. Each picked out the size that fit him best. George put on one of the coats but it was a little snug. He had to wear it anyway because his old coat was torn. Nonetheless, he felt good wearing his "new" coat. The next day, another box came that contained larger sizes, so George took one of those and his younger brother was given George's jacket. But he refused to wear it. Amidst tears rolling down his cheeks, he sobbed, "I can't wear that jacket, George already made it famous!"

Later that year, as the last day of school approached, thoughts of the big family picnic were uppermost in everyone's minds. All the families brought food to share. Softball teams were organized for the older children and games like tag and leapfrog were played by the younger ones. The climax of the day came when ice cream was dished out to everyone.

One of the men went to his car and brought out a tall cylinder. It appeared to be wrapped in a padded, khaki, blanket-like cover. Straps held the cylinder closed tight. The children crowded around as one of the teachers removed the straps and unfolded the top flaps to reveal the big, frozen treat. One of the adults dipped a scoop in water and began to dig out the ice cream. Initially it was hard as rock, but as the afternoon passed, the ice cream became soft as it melted. That didn't matter; it was delicious. Alvin was large for his age and when his turn came to get ice cream, the man dipping the cones said, "Oh, here's a big man." Then Alvin received three or four scoops while the smaller boys just received one. That night, the path to the outhouse was well worn as his stomach wasn't used to such rich food.

For many years, when summer vacation started, the Blackdeer family moved to the Wisconsin Dells for summer work at Parson's Trading Post and Indian Ceremonial. It was exciting to be with other children. They lived in a tent just large enough to sleep in and cooked their meals over a campfire.

The older members of the family had special roles in the ceremonial

Cecelia Blackdeer

each evening. One scene which impressed the tourists was the "Indian Love Call." An Indian in full dress stood singing high up on the riverbank. Donald Blackdeer, portraying Hiawatha, paddled an Indian canoe to the shore under a bright spotlight. A beautiful, young Indian princess, played by Cecelia Blackdeer, waited on shore next to a large tepee. She joined Hiawatha in the canoe and they faded back into the darkness of the river as the spotlight went out.

Other family members were accomplished dancers. They participated in traditional dances such as the "Welcome Dance," the "Snake Dance," the "Green Corn Dance" and many others. The highlight of the powwow was the contest dancing.

Alvin and his young friends often ran up to groups of tourists to ask if they would like to watch the children dance. Of course the tourists couldn't resist these young Indians, so they usually collected quite a crowd. After the performance, one of the onlookers passed a hat and then tossed the coins to the children. The dancers scrambled to pick up the change, especially the silver coins. The children were allowed to keep the coins. In addition, each child received ten dollars per summer for dancing in the nightly ceremonials. This money was given to their parents.

After the children picked up their coins, they ran to Parson's Trading Post to buy ice cream. It was here that Alvin ate his first ice cream bar on a stick. His mouth watered just thinking about them. He had enjoyed ice cream at school picnics but these ice cream bars were a double treat because they were covered with chocolate. A bar didn't last long—a couple of gulps and Alvin was ready for his next one.

During the day, Alvin's sister Cecelia worked in Parson's Trading Post behind the ice cream counter. To Alvin's dismay and disappointment, Cecelia would only allow him to buy one ice cream bar a day. As the summer wore on, though, he learned to watch when his sister took a break so he could go back for another bar.

Alvin continued to love ice cream throughout his life. So often, as he savored the delicious frozen treat, he reminisced about the days when a nickel ice cream bar on a stick meant so much to a big little Indian boy.

Alvin's father, Charlie Blackdeer, as a trick rider with his horse, Snowball

CHAPTER FOURTEEN

A TRUE FISH STORY

Alvin's mother and father used to crave muskrat, turtles, carp and all kinds of other fish, so Alvin and his brothers went hunting or fishing as often as possible to put fresh meat on the table.

One day, they left the house early in the morning, wearing their clamp-type ice skates. Shoe skates were unheard of in those days. To put on clamp skates, you had to open the lever under the skate, attach it to your shoe and push the lever down until it fit. To keep your feet in place on the skate, you had to fasten on horse harness straps that tied across the toes and heel.

That day, the boys skated down the Black River, past the Old Indian Camp. They skated still further down to where the big culvert is now and turned to head out toward the Mississippi River. They went way out, as they planned to set traps. Besides the traps, they also had an ax, turtle hooks and other things that might be needed, all tossed into the box on the little sled they were pulling. If they didn't use the sled, each boy would have had to carry a gunnysack full of the supplies.

Alvin was pulling the sled as they went out toward Sunset Point, a river entryway right across the Mississippi River from Dakota, Minnesota. At that time, there were still some islands with houses on them out there. One of the islands had an artesian well that ran constantly by pressure under the ground. They always stopped there for a drink of water when they were close by.

While they were drinking this day, the boys heard the loud, frightening sound of ice cracking between them and their way home. They could see parts of the ice moving menacingly like a miniature earthquake. Ice and water erupted from the depths of the lake. A long mass of ice stood up on end and crashed down on the frozen lake. The boys saw icicles, broken ice crystals and dust rise up like a cloud as the line of ice crashed and broke apart. Gigantic chunks of ice disappeared as the mass dipped down under the water and shot up again. Some of the ice chunks were eighteen to twenty feet long and they formed a huge ice dam.

The boys panicked about how they would get back home. Were they trapped on the wrong side of the ice? They knew they had to find a place to cross back but were afraid it would become dark soon and they wouldn't be able to see. The boys started back.

They were looking for a place where the ice jam was safe enough for them to jump over or crawl across, when they saw an area where there was lots of movement. To their surprise, heaps of carp, sheephead, buffalo, pickerel and other fish that had been under the ice were caught in the movement of the ice jam and thrown up onto the ice. As a result, all the boys had to do was go pick them up! The fish were all wiggling—very much alive!

After several tries, they found a place to cross with their sled box packed full of fish. Their folks were astonished to see all the fish as the boys hadn't brought any poles or spears with them.

Alvin lived on the banks of this water all his life and that was the first and only time he ever witnessed the making of an ice jam as grotesque as that one.

CHAPTER FIFTEEN

LIVING OFF THE LAND

During the Depression, the Blackdeer children helped put food on the table by hunting and trapping. Each morning before school, they walked miles up the Black River to check their traps. Nothing was ever wasted. The trapped animals, such as muskrat and beaver, provided meat for their table and furs that were sold to support the family.

On weekends or holidays when the Blackdeer boys weren't chopping wood or doing chores, they went hunting. This was before the area was made into a lake, so the bottom lands were covered with woods and small rivers.

Whenever they saw mink tracks go into the base of a large tree where roots were exposed along the river bank, they ran home and got Phoebe, their friendly little scrub dog.

Whoever was home at the time (usually Alvin's mother and sisters) grabbed a club or stick. Then they, together with the dog, headed for the tree. One person held the dog while the rest started poking into the tree with their sticks. When they got close to it, the mink made a run for it. If the mink managed to miss their nearby traps, the person holding Phoebe let the dog loose. Phoebe never failed to catch and kill the valuable mink. A mink hide brought a good price in those days, so Phoebe was worth her weight in gold as she helped the Blackdeer family survive the Depression.

Caroline Decorah Blackdeer was a large, six-foot-tall woman. Her usual dress was a long, dark skirt and a gray oxford shawl with long fringes. Sometimes her head was covered with a dark scarf.

Charlie and Caroline did most of their grocery shopping at the Van Loon General Merchandise Store in Midway. They always went shopping together and seldom brought any of the children. In the early thirties, Caroline spoke broken English, but preferred to speak in her native tongue. When shopping for groceries in those days, you usually handed the clerk your list of needed supplies and waited for him to gather the groceries from around the store. Caroline walked around the room, sometimes pointed to items, and then told her husband what she wanted. Charlie relayed the spoken list to John Van Loon, the store owner, who gathered up the supplies.

Charlie Blackdeer was a great fisherman and hunter. When he'd fish, Charlie watched air bubbles in the water and knew just where to throw his spear. When he trapped, he always came home with more muskrats than his neighbors ever did.

Back in the thirties, the federal government gave sheep to Indian families to help feed their families. The number they received depended on the number of children in the family. The Blackdeers were given six sheep. The boys thought the sheep were so playful and cute, they convinced their parents to keep them for pets rather than eat them.

The boys tied the sheep to the chicken coop, but one by one they got loose and disappeared. The sheep wandered through the bottom lands and the woods on the prairie. Every once in a while, a hunter stopped by to report seeing a sheep at the edge of one of the rivers that ran through the swamp land, like Broken Gun, Black Snake or French Slough. Many times the sheep wandered as far north as Lytles. Invariably, by the time the boys got to where the sheep had been seen, they were gone again.

One Armistice Day, Robert, Alvin and their father were out hunting

The Blackdeers: Charlie and Caroline on the left, Harold and Nellie on the right

snapping turtles. Alvin stayed with their boat, while Charlie and Robert hunted the river banks. They used regular turtle hooks, which consisted of a long pole with a hook on one end. They poked into the mud on the banks to locate the turtles. When they hit a turtle's back, it sounded like a drum. Sometimes five or more turtles nested together. When they found a nest, Charlie and Robert hooked the turtles one at a time and dragged them out of the mud.

That day, a big storm came up suddenly. It didn't affect the turtle hunters who were on land, but Alvin thought he better get their twenty-foot, flat-bottomed boat up on the shore. Just then, Alvin heard a strange sound, like the "bah" of an injured sheep. He looked around and out toward the lake. He spotted a duck hunter in a skiff drifting out into the open water toward Gibb Flats. Their father told Alvin and Robert to go help the man.

Sitting side by side, fighting to paddle through the stormy waves, Alvin and Robert finally reached him. The frightened man had given up. His boat paddle was broken and the skiff was drifting with the current out into the lake. He was still calling for help but was so hoarse from yelling that they couldn't make out what he was saying. No wonder Alvin thought it was his lost sheep!

When the boys pulled up behind him, he hadn't seen them coming, so it was as if they had come from nowhere in answer to a prayer. The man didn't say a word. They pulled the skiff, with the man right in it, into their big, flat boat and brought him back safely to shore. He got out and walked away without looking back or even saying thank you. He left his gun, boat and decoys behind and never returned to claim them. That may have been his last hunting trip because he was never seen again.

On another occasion, Alvin and his brothers went turtle hunting. They caught two gunnysacks full of snapping turtles—there must have been seven or eight turtles. When they got home, Alvin's father had the boys bring the turtles into the house so they wouldn't freeze (frozen turtles could not be sold). Charlie tied the gunnysacks securely, double-checked the knots and put them in a corner of the kitchen.

That evening, Stella Greendeer, Lizzy Johnson and Nathan Bird

*Alvin's sister White Dove,
Beatrice (Blackdeer) LaMere*

*Caroline Blackdeer
and Stella Greendeer*

came to visit. As was common then, when people went visiting they also stayed overnight. It was a full house that night. There were fourteen people altogether: two girls, seven boys and five adults. In a room off the kitchen, Stella slept in the bed, while Floyd, Alvin, Nathan and Lizzy all slept on the floor.

During the night, the turtles bit an opening in one of the gunnysacks. In a nice warm house, they became active and started to creep around the room. A bloodcurdling scream erupted from Lizzy, "Something's crawling on my blanket!"

Alvin recalled, "All hell broke loose. There was no electricity so we were all groping in the dark. Pa lit the lamps and started rounding up the snapping turtles. Floyd and I started laughing, but it was no laughing matter. We were lucky no one was bitten. Ma was really angry. She threatened to kick both the turtles and Pa out!"

After the turtles were caught and everyone settled down, there wasn't a person who didn't sleep with one eye open that night, just in case. Turtles were never kept inside the Blackdeer home again.

CHAPTER SIXTEEN

TEACHING THE BLOODHOUNDS

C harlie Blackdeer was well-known and well-liked. One of his friends was George Brooks, who later became nationally known because of his ability to track criminals and find lost people. George and his bloodhounds were especially good at finding people who had drowned. The bloodhounds followed tracks, often to the river's edge, and the body was found.

In order to train his dogs, George paid each of the Blackdeer boys a nickel to run several miles, crossing fields, roads and the river bank, leaving a trail for the dogs to follow. He only let them do this about once a month so the dogs wouldn't get used to their scents.

George had a brother, Archie, who was something of a character. He was a very likable person to some, but not always to others. The Blackdeer boys all thought the world of him. One winter, Archie came to their home when the entire Blackdeer family was down sick in bed. As a kindness, he trudged through deep snowdrifts all the way to Midway (two miles there and two miles back) to get flour, potatoes and other staple goods for them. Archie returned with the groceries in a gunnysack slung over his shoulder. He even brought candy for the kids.

They never forgot his kindness.

Years ago on Brice Prairie, there was no electricity anywhere near the Blackdeer home and there were very few neighbors. People were scattered so far apart that many days the mailman was the only one to drive past their home. Grass grew between the wheel tracks.

In the thirties, Alvin Nessler was hired as a new La Crosse County highway patrolman. He used mules with road graders and snowplows on the dirt roads. When snow blocked the roads, he resorted to using a tumble bucket and mule to clear a path for cars to pass through. There were no snowplows. Often the Blackdeers were stranded for four or five days at a stretch. As soon as a path was cleared, the children once again made their long walk to school. During those snow days their teacher stayed at the George Roellich farm, which was the house closest to the school.

CHAPTER SEVENTEEN

CHRISTMAS PAST

This is a story that Alvin told me in 1986. I recorded his words and submitted them to the La Crosse Tribune Christmas Story Contest. The story won third prize.

"Christmas was an exciting time for me as a little child. John Ash used to come out on Brice Prairie, load his car with us Indian kids and bring us to a church program in La Crosse. We didn't go for the religious part of the program. We'd sit through any program just to get a bag of candy, an apple and an orange!

"Those were the days (1930's) when my mother, the Funmakers, Little Bears, Kate Miner, Mrs. Whitedog and the Thunderchiefs gathered at the Fourth Street entrance of the Doerflinger store to sell their baskets. It was the time of Al Capone and John Dillinger, so my mother insisted we, her youngest children, would have to spend the day under her watchful eye so we wouldn't be kidnapped. We'd have to get up early and load the baskets. Mother always bundled them up in a big sheet. As any normal kids, we were bored stiff not being able to play, so we walked and walked, always within sight of my mother. We memorized the beautiful window displays and peeked into Doerflinger's

Selling baskets at Doerflinger's

Christmas was an exciting time for me as a little child. John Ash used to come out on Brice Prairie, load his car with us Indian kids and bring us to a church program in La Crosse. We didn't go for the religious part of the program (We'd sit through any program just to get a bag of candy, an apple and an orange!).

Blackdeer

Those were the days when my mother, the Funmakers, Little Bears, Kate Miner, Mrs. Whitedog and the Thunderchiefs gathered at the Fourth Street entrance of the Doerflinger store to sell their baskets. It was the time of Al Capone and John Dillinger, so my mother insisted we, her youngest children, would have to spend the day under her watchful eye so we wouldn't be kidnapped. We'd have to get up early and help load the baskets. Mother always bundled them up in a big sheet. As any normal kid, we were bored stiff not being able to play, so we walked and walked, always within sight of my mother. We memorized the beautiful window displays and peeked into Doerflinger's through the door. Many a time we were scolded by my mother for being in the way of Doerflinger customers.

In those days, the one and only real Santa Claus appeared in La Crosse and he sat inside at Doerflinger's. One day he caught my eye and motioned for me to come to him — instead I was afraid of him and hurried to hide behind my mother. The only times I had seen Santa was in pictures flying away in the sky in his sleigh with reindeers so I was afraid he, too, might kidnap me and take me in his sleigh. My dad didn't like the idea of my being afraid, so he grabbed me by the hand and took me up to see him. Santa gave me a bag of candy and surprised me with a kiss on my forehead.

There is another memory of those days I've saved until last. When we stood at the Doerflinger doorway, we could see a beautiful lady behind the candy counter. She wore fancy clothes and even wore lipstick. She used to bring me a piece of candy — one in the morning and one in the afternoon. I suppose she felt sorry for the little Indian boys who stayed outside all day long. She was the one who brought me Christmas cheer. I have never forgotten her — so wherever you are, Merry Christmas, Candy Lady.

through the door. Many a time my mother scolded us for being in the way of Doerflinger customers.

"In those days, the one-and-only real Santa Claus appeared in La Crosse and he sat inside at Doerflinger's. One day he caught my eye and motioned for me to come to him. Instead, I was afraid of him and hurried to hide behind my mother. The only times I had seen Santa were in pictures flying away in the sky with reindeer so I was afraid he, too, might kidnap me and take me away. My dad didn't like the idea of my being afraid, so he grabbed me by the hand and took me up to see him. Santa gave me a bag of candy and surprised me with a kiss on my forehead.

"There is another memory of those days I've saved until last. When we stood at the Doerflinger doorway, we could see a beautiful lady behind the candy counter. She wore fancy clothes and even lipstick! She used to bring me a piece of candy, one in the morning and one in the afternoon. I suppose she felt sorry for the little Indian boys who stayed outside all day long. She was the one who brought me Christmas cheer. I have never forgotten her. So, wherever you are, Merry Christmas, Candy Lady."

CHAPTER EIGHTEEN

A BOX OF CANDY

This story was recorded as Alvin told it to me.

"Mary Lou De Boer was my first and only true puppy love. She was a year or two younger than I. She lived over where the Con De Boer farm was, which is now where the buffalo are that are owned by Marcus and Sarazan. That place has so many memories for me as a kid. We were always together. We walked to school holding hands and we'd even spend recess together. After school I'd walk her home. Sometimes we'd stand for awhile with our ears on a pole listening to the music of the electricity. I was nine. Mary Lou was seven.

"At their farm home, there was a wagon parked in the back that contained their firewood. There was a back entrance to their kitchen and her job was to fill the wood box. Right in back of the wagon was a clothesline which you had to keep an eye on or you'd strike it as you were getting off the wagon. One night I was over there. Of course I was on cloud nine. I had a big armload of wood and jumped off the back of the wagon and struck my chin on the clothesline, knocking my feet from under me. I lit flat on my back with a pile of wood on top of me, which knocked the wind out of me. I couldn't cry, as much as I wanted to, because of Mary Lou. She kept asking, 'Are you hurt?' She took the wood off me as I tried to get my breath. It was just one of those deals when you are trying to be a man but you are just a kid. I left for home as soon as I could get away and cried all the way home. Nobody saw me but I guess I cried more from embarrassment than from pain.

"Another time, Mary Lou and I were sliding down a hill. That particular day we were sliding on a homemade toboggan—just an old sign or piece of tin. She somehow fell off at the bottom of the hill and got hurt. The older kids brought her up the hill and took her to the doctor, where he put her foot in a cast.

"She missed school for a week or so. I missed her terribly, being that she was my one-and-only girlfriend. During this time, I had saved a few nickels and dimes. My folks knew I had a crush on my little friend so they felt sorry for me when I asked them to take my money and buy her a box of candy as they were going downtown to sell some hides. Of course they had to add to my money to buy that small box of candy, but I thought it was really something. I was going to be able to give Mary Lou a gift!

"That night, when my folks were going grocery shopping in Midway, I got off at her home to visit for a few minutes and surprise her with the box of candy. As it was wintertime, I was only allowed to stay until they came back from shopping so I could ride home with them.

"I knocked on the door, feeling great. Then I heard a lot of voices. I was invited in and there was my Mary Lou surrounded by lots of company and four or five big boxes of candy and a couple of cakes. One even said 'Get Well Soon' on it. I felt so, I don't know what to say, but my box of candy looked so cheap and tiny. Of course Mary Lou made a big fuss over it, saying it was pretty and how nice I was to come and bring her a present. Then she offered me a chocolate from one of the boxes. I could have died! I couldn't even talk after seeing such a fancy box of candy. I just wanted to get out of there. It wasn't only the big box; some were even covered with gold and silver tin foil! That was the only night I was happy to leave my little girlfriend and go home."

CHAPTER NINETEEN

PLAYMATES

W hen Alvin was in third or fourth grade, he had many neighborhood friends who gathered to play with him and his brother, Floyd. Some of them were Charlotte Trapp, Mary Lou De Boer, Laverne "Zooie" Zumach, Betty and Kenny Smith, Leo Greeno and Gloria Woods. Another one was Betty Kriesel, who was such a nice looking girl that, according to Alvin, she looked just like Sonja Henie, the ice skating movie star. There were many more children that Alvin just didn't remember. All of these children were white.

When Alvin was young, Indian kids were typically very superstitious. Their folks brought them up to be cautious—not to be afraid in general, but they told them things that automatically scared them. One such thing was that they were never to play hide-and-seek at night. Being all their friends were white, Alvin and Floyd paired up with a friend and felt it was all right to play at De Boers' farm because they had a big lawn light so it was never dark there. Alvin and Floyd never paired up with each other at night.

The whole neighborhood congregated at De Boers and spent lots of wonderful evenings together. In the winter, they went ice skating on the lakes between Midway and the farm and down by the railroad tracks. During warmer months, they played hide and seek.

One particular night, they were playing and saw Laverne Zumach running with his partner to hide. Floyd and his partner, with Alvin and his partner, Mary Lou, were at the home base and had to holler out "Zooie, we see you behind the woodshed" or "by the barn" or wherever they were. That meant Zooie and his partner were automatically caught and out of the game. This night, they spotted Zooie as he stuck his head out of the woodshed, a good half block away. Alvin said, "Floyd, look at Zooie sticking his head out. See, he's doing it again. Let's get him!" Floyd and Alvin were standing near a pigpen, so Floyd reached down and picked up a muddy corn cob. It was the perfect weight to throw for a long distance. The woodshed was a long way off, but by coincidence, when Floyd wound up to throw, Zooie looked out again. The corn cob got there just as Zooie stuck his head out. Floyd scored a direct hit on Zooie's head. Zooie disappeared.

He had a girl for a partner so he didn't dare cry but he was sizzling mad. If the girls hadn't been there, surely there could have been a fight. At that age, though, they all tried to be gentlemen in front of the girls. The next day at school, Zooie had a black-and-blue bruise on his forehead. He never told the teacher how he got it.

The bonds of friendship established by these children on Brice Prairie during the thirties have been maintained throughout the years.

CHAPTER TWENTY

SWAB JOCKEY

I n 1943, Alvin enlisted in the United States Navy and served his country for the next four and a-half years. He returned home on leave following his graduation from boot camp at the Great Lakes Naval Training Station. His parents hadn't opened any of his mail while he was gone. In the batch of mail that lay waiting for him when he got home were letters from the La Crosse County No. 2 Draft Board inquiring why he hadn't answered his draft notice.

One afternoon while enjoying his leave, Alvin put on comfortable civilian clothes and went outside. He was raking the lawn when a La Crosse County deputy sheriff saw him, stopped and arrested him for draft evasion. Alvin told him he was on leave from the Navy, but the deputy wouldn't even look at the papers he was carrying. The deputy just said, "Tell it to the judge!"

No explanation was good enough, so Alvin got into the squad car and was taken directly to court in front of Judge Ahlstrum. Now, he thought, at least someone would listen to him. When Alvin showed the judge his leave papers, the deputy was given a good tongue lashing, right there in front of the court. With the deputy's apology, Judge

Alvin Blackdeer
U.S. Navy, 1943–1948

Ahlstrum gave Alvin a dollar, adding "Sorry, sailor. Go buy the best drink in town!" And he did!

While in the navy, Alvin traveled all over the South Pacific, Australia, New Zealand, China, the Philippines, Italy, England, France, Sweden and ports on the Mediterranean. He saw the world, but mostly from a porthole. He served most of his navy time on the USS Tangier. There were no leaves to travel inland during World War II unless he was on special detail.

Alvin's first tour of overseas duty was in the South Pacific, hauling troops on the USS Tangier, running the boats to the beachheads. On the island of Leyte in the Philippines, once the men were landed on the beach, Alvin decided to walk on solid ground before returning to the ship. He went ashore and walked inland. He could hear the sound of rifles and machine guns. Airplanes were bombing as a full-fledged invasion was in process, but not in the immediate area.

Alvin was on a highway near the beach when a sight he had seen somewhere before appeared before his eyes. There stood a statue of a Boy Scout in uniform. He had seen it either in a geography book at school or in a magazine. The sight was so familiar to him, even though it had been marred with bullets from the fighting. He found out later the statue had been donated by the Boy Scouts of America to the Boy Scouts of the Philippines.

While in Manila, several months before the war ended, groups of army officers and navy admirals were assigned to go to Bataan and Corregidor. They needed boats for transport, so a fleet was directed to pull up to the landing dock. Alvin was manning one of the boats. When he tried to put the boat in reverse, the clutch didn't catch, so he was motioned to have the next boat take his position. He watched as the other boat loaded its passenger, and it was the most familiar person in Manila: General Douglas Mac Arthur.

After completing a job on Samoi, it wasn't possible for everyone to return to the ship, so the rest of the crew put up tents on shore in the dark. When morning came, those sailors found they had been sleeping in a cemetery. Were they ever glad to get back to the ship!

Alvin was also a master-at-arms (naval policeman) and guarded naval and marine prisoners. One day it started to rain, which was a very common event in the South Pacific. As far as the eye could see, there were trucks filled with bombs supplying the airplanes that were hopping back and forth from Emiru Island (between New Guinea and Wake Island) to the Philippines.

When Alvin hopped into the nearest truck to escape the rain, the driver recognized him as an Indian and asked if he knew Donald Blackdeer. Of course Alvin knew Donald; he was Alvin's brother! The driver turned out to be Clayton (Punk) Holter from Holmen—Alvin's hometown, you might say!

Another time, Alvin was in Hollywood, California, at the Stage Door Canteen, a famous World War II USO building, when he saw signs posted for each state in the U.S. He went over to the Wisconsin area and who should he meet but a soldier with a big smile on his face. He asked if Alvin was a Blackdeer. This time it was Francis Gaarder from Holmen.

Four of the Blackdeer brothers were in the service at the same time: Donald was in the 32nd Division of the Army Field Artillery, Robert was in the 506th Engineer Company, Floyd was in the Air Corps, and Alvin was in the U.S. Navy. Marlin joined the Army right after the war and was a guard at the Nuremberg trials.

Alvin crossed the equator twice and also the international dateline during his navy years. He saw two Tuesdays and two Sundays in a row. He became a "trusty shellback" according to a certificate he received for his travels.

Just before World War II ended, Alvin left the USS Tangier and was attached to the 7th Admiral Flag 7th Fleet based in Manila. They were off the edge of Bataan and Corregidor where General Wainwright had to surrender all the troops under his command in the Philippines. Before they surrendered, they burned all their paper money so it wouldn't fall into the hands of the Japanese invaders. They also had a lot of huge, silver coins, called Philippine pesos, that were buried in the ocean off Corregidor.

Alvin was in Manila when the atomic bomb was dropped. The U.S. forces were getting ready for the invasion of Japan, so all the fleets,

Blackdeer brothers: Floyd (Air Corps), Alvin (Navy), Donald (Army), Robert (Army)

troop transports and men were assembled in the Manila Harbor.

Alvin ran a landing craft media (LCM), a big boat, as part of an operation to collect the silver coins from the bottom of the harbor. The LCM was able to haul an army tank or a couple of army trucks. It was also the type of boat used for invasion forces because it had a bow ramp that fell down for easier unloading. Alvin had a truck in the back of the LCM and one in the middle. He ran the boat with a two-man crew, an engineer and a seaman, who lowered the front end. Three LCMs were assigned to the detail; each was loaded with trucks and a crane on a barge. Using magnets, shovels and scoops on the cranes, they scraped the bottom of the harbor to get the silver. The money was

Piece of Alvin's collar carried by his mother at Indian ceremonies

loaded into the trucks on each boat until they were full. Then the LCMs returned to Manila Bay, dropped their ramps, unloaded the trucks, reloaded with empty trucks and returned to repeat the process.

Each truck had its own army officer as a security guard to watch over the operation. They had rifles and stood on top of the cab of each truck watching everyone who worked around the money. Once the LCM was anchored, Alvin could do anything he wanted until it was time to leave. He usually read a book as he waited for the unloading to be completed.

Standing in the high turret position, after the final unloading, Alvin was getting ready to return to Corregidor when he looked down and spotted something shimmering beneath the shallow water. He got down from the turret, walked over to the boat's edge and decided to jump into the water to retrieve whatever it was. His reward for getting wet was three silver pesos that must have fallen off a truck while unloading. He valued these souvenirs so much that he sent them home to his mother and two sisters. Whatever happened to them, he never knew, for he never saw them again.

All through his service, Alvin knew he would return home as he was protected by an amulet in the war bundle he kept with him at all times. His family and friends prayed for his safe return. All mothers of servicemen were proud of their sons. Whenever there were big Indian events like feasts or medicine dances, the mothers took a part of their sons' uniforms and either attached it to a pole or sewed it on a blanket so they could carry it as they danced. These mothers always made sure the insignias from their sons' uniforms were easily visible. After the war, Alvin found his insignia patch and the star from the corner of his dress blues collar—all with strings attached to them. He knew then that these were the parts of his uniform his mother had carried with her while she danced and prayed for his safe return.

Once, on shore duty in Italy, Alvin was riding in an army jeep when it tipped over. He was pinned under the rear part of the jeep. The circulation in his legs was cut off for several hours and resulted in a permanent injury. In the South Pacific, he contracted malaria, which plagued him throughout the rest of the war years and often as a civilian.

CHAPTER TWENTY-ONE

RAILROAD MEMORIES

Alvin was probably one of the youngest "old-timers" employed by the Chicago, Burlington and Quincy (CB&Q) Railroad. He received his promotion to engineer in 1957, when it was necessary to know how to operate both the steam engine and the new diesel engines. Alvin was firing engines when the men wore neckerchiefs to protect themselves from hot cinders, not just as part of the uniform.

He began his railroad career when he hired on with the Milwaukee Road in 1948. He joined the Burlington line in 1951. A highly prized possession in the Blackdeer home is the plaque commemorating the International Safety Award from the Brotherhood of Locomotive Firemen and Engineers to Alvin in 1959 for his part in stopping Train No. 81 when the engineer, Henry Cahape, died at the controls. The award was presented to him by the governor of Wisconsin, Gaylord Nelson, in Madison at a banquet in Alvin's honor.

The following is one of Alvin's most memorable railroad stories.

"Hey, Chief, your buddy just got shot," the head brakeman shouted to Alvin as the CB&Q Train No. 88 departed from La Crosse for Savanna, Illinois, on that fateful Friday, November 22, 1963.

*One of the last scheduled
runs of the Burlington
steam engine*

"I just couldn't believe what I was hearing," said Alvin, a retired Burlington Northern engineer, as he recalled the day that remained so vivid in his memory. "President Kennedy had been shot down by a sniper's rifle in Dallas. I didn't know if he was dead or alive.

"We lost radio contact with the La Crosse Depot and Prairie du Chien didn't have any news. When we pulled into Dubuque, the train dispatcher told us that our forty-six-year-old president, John F. Kennedy, had been shot to death by a hidden assassin with a high-powered rifle." Alvin learned later that Lee Harvey Oswald had been arrested for questioning. Oswald was an ex-marine who had recently returned from Russia.

Alvin went on to Savanna, where he learned more details. As we watched television that evening, seeing over and over again the pictures of the Dallas parade and the shooting, he recalled the times he had spent during the 1960 Kennedy presidential campaign with various members of the Kennedy family. As pictures of Rose Kennedy, the president's mother, were flashed across the nation, Alvin remembered the day he met this lovely lady when she was campaigning for her son in Wisconsin. Then there was Robert "Bobby" Kennedy, who came to the La Crosse airport where so many people came to meet him before he went to speak at various local functions. Eunice Shriver, the president's sister, was another enthusiastic supporter whom he met while she was campaigning in La Crosse.

Alvin was one hundred percent behind this young man who was running for the highest office in the country because Kennedy's voting record in the U.S. Senate favored legislation that benefited minorities and veterans.

When JFK was to be in La Crosse, Alvin was the commander of the Winnebago Indian Veterans Association. Veterans groups at that time could not support anyone for political office, but as Winnebago Indian veterans, they could honor JFK as a great war hero because of his heroic deeds when he saved his World War II crew on the PT 109. So with this in mind, Alvin and his fellow Winnebago veterans, Wilbur Blackdeer and LaVern Carrimon, presented JFK with a clam-shell neckpiece and an eagle feather war bonnet on behalf of the Veterans Association. Kennedy

Alvin as engineer on the Burlington Northern

was also made an honorary chief of the Winnebago Nation and given the name *Cho Ni Gah*, meaning "the leader." In acknowledging the gifts, Kennedy said the next time he watched a western on TV, he'd have to root "for our side."

Alvin had the privilege of accompanying the Kennedy caravan to different parts of the state with his sound truck. As a remembrance, he was given several highly prized records that he had used on his sound truck, including "High Hopes," which had been recorded by Frank Sinatra as a campaign song for Kennedy.

While reminiscing about the events, Alvin stated there never had been and never would be another John F. Kennedy. The nation lost a good man but the minorities lost a good friend.

Alvin and Wilbur Blackdeer with Presidential Candidate John F. Kennedy. Kennedy is presented with a war bonnet, necklace, and the name "Cho Ni Gah" during a ceremony making him an honorary chief of the Winnebago Nation.

CHAPTER TWENTY-TWO

A LEGEND OF THE WIGWAM

During the summer of 1966, Alvin and I took a short trip to the Wisconsin Dells. We visited the Indian Village where Fritz Greendeer had a souvenir shop. We also stopped to see Alvin's sister, Beatrice LaMere, at the village. Next we went to Parson's Trading Post. Here, Duane Council and his mother welcomed Alvin as he had been their friend for many years. He sang "The Maple Sugar Song" with Duane's mother as she tapped on the counter to keep time with the song. It was here Alvin purchased a colorful Indian sewing basket that he gave me after we became officially engaged to be married.

Then we took a beautiful scenic drive on a rustic road, where the pine trees grew right up next to the pavement, and ended up at the Winnebago Indian Museum. Before we entered the museum, Alvin showed me a *wickiup*, or wigwam, that tourists could visit. He led the way inside. It was like a big bowl turned upside down. The home was made of saplings that formed its shell. The outside was covered with bark. Sometimes, Alvin said, wigwams were covered with hides. Inside, it was a large comfortable room. Alvin told me the fire was built in the center of the wigwam and the smoke curled right out through the top. At times, even in the bitter Wisconsin winter, the room would become unbearably hot.

As we walked out the entryway and back to the path leading to the museum, a couple of older Indian women grinned at us while another put her hand over her mouth and giggled.

Alvin then introduced me to Roger and Bernice Tallmadge, who owned the museum. I asked Bernice what was so funny to those women, and she explained that when a brave takes his girlfriend into his wigwam they will soon be married.

Several months later, their prediction became a reality when Alvin and I stood before Rev. Mitchell Whiterabbit in front of a glowing fire in the fireplace at Alvin's home, taking our vows to become man and wife and be faithful to one another until death would part us.

I had been a widow for seven years when Alvin came into my life. My time was spent between my home and six children, my job at Wettstein & Sons and the American Legion clubrooms where I served as the President of Unit 52 Auxiliary. I often played the piano there as many of the veterans and auxiliary members enjoyed singing songs of our era like "Don't Fence Me In," "Mairzy Doats," "I Left My Heart in San Francisco" and many other requested songs. One night I heard a baritone voice that drowned out everyone else singing "Chattanooga Shoe Shine Boy." He was enjoying himself, clapping his hands in time with the music. He threw his head back, arms outstretched, and even did a little shuffle as he sang "he'd charge you a nickel just to shine your shoes." He was a real entertainer. We became friends that night—because of his singing and my piano playing. When he wasn't singing, he seemed to be a quiet man—this was my first impression of Alvin. Several weeks after that, my gentleman friend and I were invited to attend Alvin's birthday party at his home on Brice Prairie. That night Alvin's girlfriend showed me her engagement ring and gave me a tour of his home. It was beautiful. I thought to myself how sad it was that his wife had only lived in her new home a few years before her death. Al and I found ourselves together a lot that night. The party was held in his basement with his brother George's band playing. There must have

Alvin and Muriel beside a wigwam

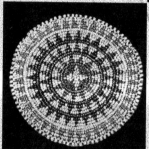

Wigwam frame

been at least thirty friends dancing, joking and just plain having a good time.

A few weeks later, Al called me and I'll never forget his words, "Would you consider going out with me?" What a different way to ask for a date. It took me by surprise. But, he had broken up with his girl-friend and couldn't get over thinking about me since his party. Well, I had enjoyed that night. He was so interesting to converse with. So I gave him directions to my home.

For the first of many nights that were to come, we went to the Blue Moon in Onalaska, where there was good food and a terrific piano bar. We both ordered steaks. He ended the evening by telling me we were going to see a lot more of each other. I asked him how he knew that. He answered, "Because you cleaned your plate." After I finally quit laughing, he explained that other women he had taken out just nibbled their food and left most of it—a big waste. So I explained that I was Norwegian and that was something we had been taught to do since childhood. He replied that Indians always did that, too. This was the first I had really thought about us being of different cultures. It was the reason he had hesitated asking me for a date. But he was such a nice person, why wouldn't I go out with him? We were both big people. We made a nice-appearing couple. We complemented each other.

Al was an engineer on the Burlington Zephyr at that time. He'd call me from Savanna, Illinois, or sometimes Minneapolis-St. Paul, to tell me when he'd be in. If he returned in the morning, he picked me up during my noon hour and we had lunch together. We became inseparable.

We took the younger children to movies. We took them on picnics or to city celebrations. We enjoyed barbershop and band concerts. We visited historic sites. We fell in love. He was kind and generous. He was an honest man. He was sincere. We had the same interests. Most of all, I loved the deep tone of his voice. He loved to talk and I loved to listen to him. We laughed a lot. He had such a good sense of humor. We con-tinued to make beautiful music together at home and for others. We enjoyed trips down country roads, stopping at little grocery stores for a loaf of bread and a ring of bologna for a roadside picnic. We were doing things his parents had done years ago.

Lake Onalaska, as viewed from the Old Indian Camp

When we announced that we were getting married, we heard remarks such as, "It'll never last," and "You'll lose all your white friends." I even heard a "friend" remark, "Her mother and father would turn over in their graves if they knew she was going to marry an Indian." Well, my dad and Al would have enjoyed swapping war stories (Dad was World War I, Al was World War II). As for my mother, she was alive and thought the world of Al. Why shouldn't she? Al had accomplished so much for a forty-year-old man, and she knew I had once more found happiness. Al had been a devoted son to his mother, doing everything he could to make her happy until the day she died. He did the same for my mother.

Yes, I sometimes thought of our differences, but so did Al. He'd tell our friends, "I wasn't prejudiced, I married a Norwegian." Always joking! Another subject we discussed was when the controversy arose about being an Indian or a Native American. Al said he was born an Indian and would remain an Indian all his life—and he did.

We used to swim in Lake Onalaska. We loved the mist of the water washing our faces as we skimmed across the lake in our motorboat.

As years went by, we enjoyed staying home more. We sat outside in our metal swing, watching the traffic on the lake or just gazing across the five miles of water to the Minnesota bluffs. We sat at our picnic table, feasted on wieners or hamburgers from the grill and waved at or conversed with old friends who walked by. We visited with our neighbors, Harold and Frances Fletcher. For exercise, we walked down to our boat landing or around Swarthout Park until the day Al could no longer keep up with me because of congestive heart failure.

We spent a lot of time in our lovely living room. He often asked me to play for him and he could still belt out the old songs. Then he sat and watched a lot of TV while I sat on the davenport next to his recliner. We talked and talked and talked. He no longer showed a lot of affection, but the look in his eyes told me every day that he loved me. He reached for my hand and I felt his strength envelop me. At times, when he was very ill, his strength gave me the courage to face whatever life was to hold for us. When I see couples touching or holding hands today, I remember, and I am envious. I only hope they appreciate each other.

Muriel, Barbara and Alvin Blackdeer (1987)

CHAPTER TWENTY-THREE

BAMBI

"She's got a great set of lungs," Dr. Jerome announced as our daughter was brought into the world on August 16, 1967. Her big, brown eyes captured my heart the moment I saw her. I was captivated by the beautiful olive complexion of this little miracle. As an inquisitive parent, I made a complete examination, marveling at all her black hair. There was even black fuzz on her tiny shoulders. I made sure she had ten fingers and ten toes, and then I noticed a dark patch that covered most of her buttocks.

"Was she injured during birth?" I asked Dr. Jerome. "No," he replied. "Eighty percent of non-white babies have different-sized Mongolian Spots somewhere on their back." When Alvin's sister, Beatrice, saw it, she nodded her head saying, "Every true Indian baby has this mark, Muriel. It will disappear as she grows." And it did. Later I was surprised to hear many young Indian mothers have been accused of child abuse because of these markings. It is understandable because such a birthmark looks like a black-and-blue bruise to people who are unaccustomed to seeing it.

When we brought our baby girl home, the crib was waiting for her.

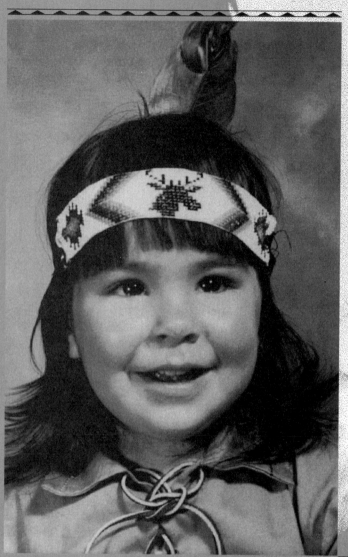

Bambi Blackdeer, age two

There was also an Indian hammock stretched from the window to the closet in the master bedroom. Alvin made the hammock with rope and a large blanket while I was in the hospital. The baby was wrapped in her own blanket and placed in the hammock. Anytime she'd start crying or fussing, the slightest movement rocked her back to sleep. I thought it was simpler and much safer for me to use the crib; so, much to the dismay of Aunt Beatrice and Alvin, the hammock was removed.

Barbara Jo (Bambi) was welcomed to the family by seven half-sisters and brothers: Gail, Richard, Robert, Harlan, Debra, David and Caroline. Both Alvin and I had experienced the sadness of the death of our former partners and seeing as we both had children by these marriages, a readymade family was waiting for the baby.

Having the name of Blackdeer, it was natural for us to call her our little "deer." Alvin kept bringing home deer pins, deer toys, bibs and clothing all bearing the name "Bambi" every time he made a railroad trip. So she became our Bambi. We wanted her to be proud of both her Norwegian and Indian heritages, so we brought her up celebrating customs of both cultures.

Pastor Berntson, at the Holmen Lutheran Church, baptized *Barbara Jo* on September 24, 1967, and Pastor Laehn confirmed her at the same church. At an Indian feast, Wilbur Blackdeer, an elder of the Winnebago tribe, gave Bambi her Indian name, *See Wi Si oo Ki Wi* (pronounced hoo wa hue gee wi), meaning "Queen of the Elks."

Alvin loved his new little girl. We always brought her with us to all Indian gatherings, as Indians have a special love for little children that I have never seen amongst white people. On Labor Day, when Bambi was only a few weeks old, we all attended the annual Labor Day Powwow at Red Cloud Park near the mission outside Black River Falls. It was Alvin's day to show off his new daughter. He insisted on carrying her at all times and I soon found out why. Alvin took our tiny baby and proudly introduced her to each of the male elders of the tribe by placing her in their arms. "She is a beautiful child," the first elder said, smiling down at our baby. After going from elder to elder, Alvin presented her to Chief John Winneshiek, who stated, "She will bring you much happiness." My heart was happy watching Alvin, the proud father, performing this old ritual.

Soon after Bambi was born, she was registered in the tribe through the tribal office in Tomah. She was given an enrollment number to verify that she would be eligible to receive tribal benefits.

When Bambi was still a tiny baby, we visited Roger Tallmadge at the Winnebago Indian Museum near the Wisconsin Dells. He was an old friend who was married to Alvin's cousin, Bernice. Roger was very respected amongst both whites and Indians. He represented Wisconsin and Governor Dreyfus at a trade mission in Saudi Arabia.

Roger asked me if anyone had presented Bambi with moccasins yet. When I said no, he replied, "Let me have the honor." Roger picked out a beautiful pair of white moccasins decorated with white and yellow seed beads. As he placed them on her tiny feet, he instructed her to always "stand straight and walk tall." Then holding her little feet in his hands, he spoke in his low, melodious voice, as if he were a prophet:

Her white moccasins will take her to

where fields are greener,

where eagles fly,

where deer is plentiful

beneath the rainbow sky.

CHAPTER TWENTY-FOUR

TIME FOR A POWWOW

very Memorial Day and Labor Day, Alvin and I, with some of our children, would travel to Black River Falls to visit Alvin's old friends and relatives at the powwow.

As we drove into the grounds, there was always a ball game in progress. Scattered throughout the park were new campers, covered trucks with cots or mattresses in the back, and tents of all sizes, some old, some brand new. Whole families would be there sharing their living quarters with friends and relatives, catching up on the news since the last powwow, and waiting for the dancing to begin.

Al and I would walk around the powwow grounds, stopping to look over the beaded jewelry, new Indian shirts, and Indian dresses made to be sold here at the powwow. Our favorite stand was run by Alvin's sister Beatrice and her friend Margaret Green. In addition to selling their crafts, they sold pop, soup, and delicious hot fry bread. There was also the main building, where women were busy preparing food for the dancing contestants and tribal members.

We stopped there to visit with Lorraine Winneshiek, and I asked her why, being the wife of the chief, she was working so hard? (We had just

Al Baldus and Bambi Blackdeer

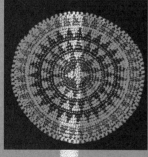

seen Chief John Winneshiek leave to fix the generator providing electricity for the grounds). She told me the chief and his family always worked for their people, not like the whites who want the people to work for them. I was impressed with her answer.

Some days were rainy so, to avoid getting their costumes wet, only a few participated in the dancing. Some days were so dry that the dancing was done in a cloud of dust. Sometimes it was just perfect, and that's when movie cameras, tape recorders, and regular cameras recorded sights and sounds of the beautiful costumes and colorful dancers, with many of the white people wishing they were Indians. Al referred to these people as belonging to the Wannabe tribe (want to be)!

The old powwow grounds had the drum pit in the center covered with pine boughs laid over a frame giving shade to the drummers. Log benches surrounded the arena for viewers to sit on. Young boys used to pick up the snakes that had crawled under the logs and run after screaming little girls—all part of the powwow fun.

One year, the people came from tribes all over the United States—an estimated five thousand people—to participate in the largest powwow ever held at Black River Falls. This was special for Bambi because it was the first powwow she had danced in with her white deerskin dress.

The Memorial Day powwow is special to veterans and their families. In the morning, flagpoles are placed and the flags of the deceased veterans are raised. Their picture is also placed on the pole.*

On Memorial Day, 1975, Alvin Baldus, Third District congressman for Wisconsin, was made an honorary member of the tribe, receiving the name *Na Di Gu*, meaning "Coming Storm." The name, given by Ralph Mann, was so the work done by Baldus would be powerful, coming with force throughout the third district, like a storm or tornado. Before the ceremony, a peace pipe and beaded American Legion emblem neckpiece were passed though the audience, where each Winnebago touched the gifts, giving them more power and signifying

---

*Richard Blackdeer, Alvin's nephew, is now in charge of Alvin's flag.

that the entire nation was presenting the gifts. After accepting the gifts, the congressman joined other veterans dancing around the arena.

Winnebagos were always interested in the federal government and their elected officials, as they depended upon the guidance of the Bureau of Indian Affairs to oversee all Indian tribes.

After the dancing stopped, we'd go back to the stands, purchase an article or two as souvenirs of the day and have one more piece of fry bread before driving through the scenic hills and valleys, through Melrose, and back to our home on Brice Prairie.

CHAPTER TWENTY-FIVE

OUR INDIAN SHOWS 1968-1987

The gymnasium, jammed to capacity with chattering, restless students sitting on the floor, instantly quieted down as the sound of a beating tom-tom boomed through the auditorium from the hallway. As the sound became louder, all eyes focused on the door as a tall Indian (to students I'm sure he looked seven feet tall) walked slowly into the room. His baritone voice sang "The Welcome Song" as he slowly made his way to the front of the auditorium. The children, with wide-open eyes, were fascinated as they looked at a real, live Indian wearing a beaded jacket and a beautiful war bonnet. This was Alvin at his best, promoting goodwill by sharing his Indian heritage with the children of the La Crosse area.

For many years we provided programs free of charge to almost every school and organization in the La Crosse area. For our first programs, I played the piano and Alvin sang both Indian and semi-classical songs. Then audiences requested more information on Indians, and we extended our programs by bringing in some of the artifacts we had adorning the walls of our home.

Bambi, Muriel and Alvin entering Oak Grove School on Brice Prairie

It usually took a day to plan the program and take down the artifacts to pack them for traveling. The process was reversed when we returned home. The artifacts were bulky. After Alvin became ill, we were unable to perform at places that weren't on the ground floor. Alvin, even then, made exceptions if Indian children attended the grade that requested the program. If he could ever do anything to make people conscious of the plight of Indians, he did it. Alvin went out of his way to make a good impression for the school so that Indian children would be proud of their heritage. He never failed to call on these children by name to come and "help" with the program, making them the envy of their classmates.

Every program was a little different, depending on who our group was for the day and where we were performing. Bambi was two years old when she started to take part in our program. She always walked proudly behind her father during the opening and took a seat at the side of the display until I called upon her.

The slow procession of the participants was an important part of the beginning, for it was at this time the audience could see the costumes close up and hear the bells and drum as they walked in. As years went by, different children joined us for the dancing.

When Alvin wanted a special show, he called on his old friend, Raymond Lowe. Ray was a terrific dancer who always looked good in his authentic Indian costume. Besides the dancing, he performed a comedy act to portray the uses of an Indian blanket and helped with the question-and-answer portion of the program. Ray and his wife, Lorraine, also brought artifacts to add to our display which made it more beautiful and informative. Together we entertained at Norskedalen near Coon Valley, Perrot State Park, for their tricentennial, the Harry J. Olson Senior Citizen Center dedication, the Oak Forest Nursing Home in Onalaska and many, many school and Scout events.

Once we held a program in our home for a group of hearing-impaired children. Their eyes and actions spoke so loudly for us. They were able to feel the vibrations of the tom-tom's sharp beat and the bell's shrill music. I think I enjoyed that program more than they did.

Alvin and Bambi performing the "Swan Dance"

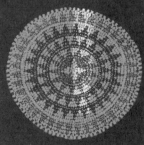

Raymond Lowe

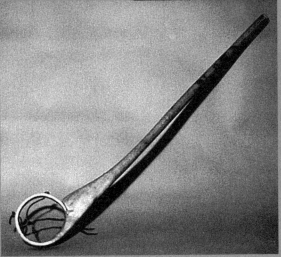

Lacrosse stick

To start the program, we always had a fast dance with Alvin explaining how the dancer had to keep time with the drum and stop at the last drumbeat. To give the dancers a rest, I started at one end of the display table and began to describe each artifact.

Alvin stood right there, so I'd describe his outfit first. His war bonnet always brought "oh's" and "ah's" from the children as he turned around to let them see the beautiful eagle feathers, the beadwork on the headband and the ribbons and rabbit fur that hung down each side. The fluffs on the feathers always brought questions, so we explained that these were added for decoration. Alvin then told us that not every person has the privilege to wear this headdress. He could because he had been a member of the Winnebago Tribal Council and had also been a modern-day warrior (a member of the U.S. Navy during World War II). The beadwork displayed on his buckskin jacket and the rosette neckpiece he wore were both made with tiny beads by his sister, Beatrice. She was well-known for this talent and was commissioned to make a wide guitar strap for Hank Williams during the 1940's.

While describing Alvin, I always stressed that Indians were no different from anyone else. They wore the same clothes as their white friends when not appearing on a program. They had to get up and go to work just like anyone else. The children were often surprised and impressed to hear that Alvin was an engineer on the Burlington Northern Railroad. I told them how one of Alvin's railroad friends brought his son over to Alvin one day when he was in the railroad yard in order to introduce the little boy to a real Indian. He looked Alvin over and said, "Dad, you're fooling me. He ain't got no feathers!"

Then I asked the audience, "What do you think I'm holding?" Very few children could ever identify the long object as a lacrosse stick. The game of lacrosse is considered one of the oldest contact sports played among Indians. Any number of players could be on the teams of this rough sport. Often the Sioux from Minnesota and the Winnebagos from Wisconsin met on the playground between the Mississippi River and the bluffs, known as Prairie La Crosse, to play this game. The game was played with sticks approximately thirty inches long. A round "racket" at the top of the stick was laced with two leather thongs that crossed to

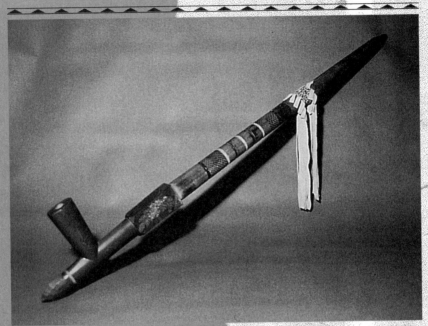

Ceremonial peace pipe

hold a wooden ball. As the ball was tossed from person to person, many an accident took place as arms and legs were hit by the lacrosse sticks or ball. It was not uncommon for players to have broken limbs by the end of the game.

Next I held before me with both my hands a ceremonial peace pipe. The beautifully carved wooden stem is twenty-eight inches long. Attached to it are twelve inches of red pipestone that make the pipe. The carvings are painted black, yellow, red and green. There are also leather fringes and beadwork on it. Most peace pipes aren't quite so elaborate and are used more often.

We had visited the national museum at Pipestone, Minnesota, where the pipestone is quarried and learned the story of pipestone from a slide show there. The stone is considered the blood of the fallen warrior and is found in veins six to eight feet beneath Mother Earth. Pipestone, Minnesota, is considered hallowed land and all Indian tribes are said to be at peace when they are at this place. Many years ago, the legend goes, two warriors met a woman there who was called White Buffalo Calf. One warrior had bad thoughts about this beautiful woman. When he tried to touch her, she disappeared. The woman then told the other warrior to tell his people to prepare a lodge for her. This was done and she returned and presented them with a pipe. They were told to think good thoughts when using this pipe. They were to pray, facing the east (the giver of life), the south (where the warm winds come from), the west (where one goes when one leaves this world) and the north (where the winds arise to give strength).

The preparation and prayers before the actual smoking of the peace pipe are the most important part of this ritual. As the pipe is passed from person to person, the smoke goes through the stem and ascends, as does the spirit's trail from life into the spirit world. Many serious decisions have been made following the smoking of the peace pipe at council fires.

An arrowhead display was shown next. Throughout the Coulee Region, farmers and nature lovers have always been able to find arrowheads in plowed fields and on islands. All this land was once inhabited by Indians for their hunting, camping and fishing grounds. Some have found ax and spearheads but most finds are the arrowheads that were used for killing small game. In the summer of 1985, Alvin was walking in our yard and found a mound of sand next to a gopher hole. There was something glittering that caught his eye, so he kicked the pile of sand and there was a perfect arrowhead that the gopher had dug up from way under the surface.

Then I described a miniature birch bark canoe. Indian families living near water are referred to as *neo quah de a shea*, meaning "living on a big river." These families have a small birch bark canoe hanging on their wall that either holds a bouquet of bittersweet or is just a decoration. This symbol is believed to keep the home safe from the waters. There are several birch bark canoes protecting our home and though flood waters have threatened our property, our home has remained safe.

Next I described all the baskets we had brought. There were large picnic baskets with covers, some market baskets and of course the sewing basket Alvin gave to me when we became engaged to be married. One of the baskets belonged to my grandmother, so it was more than sixty years old. She carried eggs in that basket from their farm to the store in Westby to trade for groceries. She had purchased it from the

Indians that were selling baskets outside the Doerflinger Store in La Crosse. I had been told that the Doerflinger Store was the only place in the city that allowed Indians to sell their goods on the street by their building. We explained that prices have really gone up on the baskets now, but

with all the work that goes into making them, they are worth it. Because of the way it is made, an Indian basket can be repaired if a strip breaks or comes loose.

The task of basket weaving is a tedious job that begins in the swamp, where the straight black ash tree is cut and dragged to the area where it is pounded until all the sap is gone. Alvin often did this for his mother. When this was done, the log separated into strips, and these strips were then divided into different lengths and widths. Some were left the natural color of the  wood, while others were dyed different colors using dyes made from weeds and berries.

Indian women often got together to make a social time with their weaving. They exchanged different colored strips while they visited and worked on their baskets. This saved them the trouble of making many different colors, as each woman made a big batch of one color to trade for other colors.

The large baskets carried quantities of food. Little girls played with the tiny baskets. These are now museum pieces. Each basket had its own identity. The women who did the weaving could recognize who made a basket by its particular design. The last basket made by Alvin's mother,  Caroline, has old-fashioned, bound handles, as she was unable to get wooden handles at the time. It is the only basket we have that was made in this manner, so our family values it highly.

Ray and Alvin took over

the program at this point to keep it moving along by doing the blanket act. Alvin announced what Ray was going to do with the blanket and Ray folded the blanket in different ways and, inserting some comedy, showed the audience a shy maiden, a cold winter night, how to carry a papoose, and an Indian runner. To close the act, he'd always fold the blanket over his arm for the long journey. He moved his head from side to side, as if watching cars go by, and stick out his thumb like a hitchhiker. It always brought a good laugh.

A contest dance was usually held so we could have audience participation. The dancer did his fancy dance and then handed a cluster of feathers or gourd to someone else so he/she could do a dance. After several children had participated, we had the class vote to see who was the best.

Continuing with the display, we showed a group of beadwork pieces on a black felt background that were mounted on an easy-to-handle stand. One of the articles in this display was a traveling feather presented to Alvin in honor of all the traveling he had done over the years as an engineer on the Burlington Northern Railroad. The presentation was made by the women of the 32nd Division Auxiliary, who sponsored the Armistice Day program honoring veterans at Camp Douglas. Other pieces in the display included beaded necklaces, an intricate beaded figure, wallets, coin purses and jewelry that were made by Beatrice La Mere, Alvin's sister. I asked Beatrice to make me a woman's neckpiece with red and white beads and a black-beaded deer. I was disappointed when I received a blue rosette with a black deer in the center, but she explained it was because I was "blue eyes" and had married her brother. After that, it became very special to me.

I always enjoyed the next part of the program because I told all about our daughter. When she was little, I'd lift her up on a table so everyone could see Bambi in her buckskin outfit. She really enjoyed being a model. It is the dream of every young Indian girl to own a white buckskin dress, so we were all overjoyed when her Aunt Beatrice consented to make such an outfit for Bambi.

Three tanned hides were used to make this beautiful outfit. Bambi was only four years old at the time, but Beatrice made the dress in true

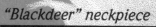

Beaded purse

"Blackdeer" neckpiece

Indian fashion as if full sized. The top was made with large scallops and worn like a cape. Every scallop was edged with red seed beadwork. The skirt was made very large and then pleated so, as the child grew, the skirt could be let out. The tedious job of cutting fringes by hand was given to Beatrice's daughters, Peachy and Brenda, with help from our niece, Rita. The fringes were attached to the outfit and beads were added to each fringe. To complete the outfit, fringed leggings were made.

Beatrice made beadwork pieces of rainbow colors and a black deer that were placed on each shoulder. She also made a matching bracelet and, of course, a headband for Bambi's eagle feather. "Earrings" were made of long, beaded strings. Bambi wore these in her hair. Another long string of beads was worn down the back of the dress. Tiny red beads were strung to make many necklaces for the front. Three rosettes of beadwork were worn as the center neckpiece. To complete the outfit, Beatrice made a lovely red shawl with long fringes that was worn over the outfit or carried on Bambi's arm. This white buckskin outfit will be handed down to other generations.

When I mentioned her beaded headband, Bambi pointed to it and listened to the story of how she got her eagle feather. It is considered a great honor for anyone to receive an eagle feather. In Winnebago tradition, the only person who can present a feather is a combat veteran. He must relate his experiences to an assembled crowd.

Bambi received her eagle feather during a ceremony at the Red Cloud Park powwow grounds near Black River Falls when she was three years old. Murray Whiterabbit, a war hero and close relative, presented the feather and told of his combat experience during World War II. The crowd sat entranced as he told of his time in the Ranger Battalion at Normandy Beach. During combat, he crept up unseen to an armored tank and threw a grenade into the turret hole. He was credited with killing six German soldiers.

Murray then stooped over and, with a big smile, placed an eagle feather in Bambi's tiny hand. In return, Alvin gave Murray a gift for honoring our daughter. To conclude the ceremony, all of Bambi's relatives joined in a round dance. Bambi held her feather in one hand and

Bambi Blackdeer

her Aunt Beatrice's hand with the other one as they all danced around the drum pit. This was a big day in the life of our little girl.

As our program continued, we rang bells of all sizes and explained how dancers wore them to add to the rhythm of their dances. We showed dried gourds that rattled and antique war clubs. The last items in our display were beautifully-decorated dresses and moccasins that were so old they were starting to fall apart. We always used bright Indian blankets to cover our display tables to make them more attractive.

The question-and-answer section of the program was always of interest to everyone. There were questions such as "What did the Indians use before paper diapers?" (milkweed) and "How come the Indians let the white people take over the country?" (Alvin's standing punch line, "Guess we had poor immigration laws!").

Our program closed with a slide show of Bambi growing up, various costumes worn by Indians during powwows, plus old friends and ancestors of the Blackdeer family.

Photographs, drawings, letters and posters all arrived several days after a program thanking us for an informative presentation. The one Winnebago word we tried to teach the students was *Pe na gee gee*, or "thank you."

*Alvin and Bambi on the day of the
Winnebago graduation banquet**

*High school graduation for an Indian was very special. For Bambi's
graduating class of Winnebagos, a banquet was held where each
graduating senior received $50 for achieving their educational goals.
All other students from high school down to preschool received a silver
dollar and a certificate to encourage them to continue to achieve
educational success. Their certificates read "Good at Baseball" or
"Good at Reading," or for younger ones, "Good at Recess!"

CHAPTER TWENTY-SIX

FAREWELL

The mirrors had been covered with cloth so there were no reflections. All of Alvin's pictures were no longer visible. All his possessions had been removed from the house.[1] The casket bearing his body was carried through the front door. Alvin had returned home for the last time.

I watched as he was placed facing west, by the windows that looked out over Lake Onalaska.[2] This was the room filled with memories.

Chairs were brought in and arranged in anticipation of friends and relatives who would soon fill our home for a last farewell. Flowers were placed all around, adding beauty and giving life to a room filled with sorrow.

---

[1] All personal effects—Alvin's guns, clothing, thermos bottle, flashlights, tools, jewelry and anything he used on a daily basis—were packed into boxes by close relatives, carried outside and placed behind the garage until the morning following the day of his burial. Even our bed and bedding were removed from the house. I requested to keep the bed. All other possessions were given to Ralph Mann and Kenny Littlegeorge, members of the Bear Clan who were in charge of the burial, and distributed to tribal members who would continue to use them. I'm glad we followed the old Indian customs throughout the funeral. Alvin wanted it that way.

[2] At an Indian burial, the head of the casket is in the east, so the person faces the west. This places his feet in the right direction to start on his last journey toward the sunset.

The flag of our country draped his coffin. The hats Alvin loved to wear were lined up inside the casket to represent the organizations he belonged to as a veteran. The Winnebago Veterans took turns serving as honor guards beside their friend at all times.

Alvin's wish was to wear a regular suit so his local friends would see him in his familiar clothes, but he also wanted to be buried in the Indian manner and follow all Indian traditions as this was the religion he followed all his life. A beautiful Indian blanket covered his shoulders, the beaded neckpiece that he wore for our programs adorned his chest and moccasins were slipped on his feet for his journey.*

I sat alone for awhile, looking at him. This man who was always so full of life now lay silently in the home he built and loved so much.

I looked at the fireplace in this very room and remembered the night we stood there, before witnesses and family, and repeated our marriage vows. "'Til death do us part." The day was here. Death had parted us. Never again would I hear the voice I loved. Never again would I hold the hand that radiated strength to me when I needed him. Never again would his eyes speak to me of secrets only we would share. Never again would his laughter echo through the house.

The men in charge of the burial gathered around Alvin. They spoke in Winnebago and gave Alvin instructions on how he was to go on his journey.

A friend had related to me that the Great Spirit had once given the Indian a flower to guard before placing him on earth. The flower was to be returned when he returned to the Great Spirit. The flower was tobacco. Bambi had been instructed to get blue-and-white cloth. This square of material was filled with tobacco and placed in Alvin's hands to take back as his offering to the Great Spirit.

Tears gathered in my eyes and started to overflow as the saddest Indian song I've ever heard was chanted. "Do not cry, Muriel," a gentle woman's voice whispered in my ear. "It will make his spirit not want to

---

*The moccasins Alvin wore were made of deerskin that was tanned in the old Indian way by his niece, Rita Blackdeer. Alma Miner cut the moccasins from the hide and was assisted in sewing them by Lilah Blackdeer.

leave you." Another woman whispered, "You must be brave." I wanted to cry out that I was a white woman and I didn't know all the Indian customs! I didn't want my husband to leave me! Instead, I closed my eyes and quietly prayed, "Dear Lord, help me." I heard sobs from my sister. An older Indian woman told her, "Cry for your sister, but not for Alvin!"

Friends and relatives continued to walk past the casket. I heard myself say, "Thank you for coming," but I don't recall to whom I was talking.

"Take your children and say goodbye," I was instructed. For the last time, Caroline, Bambi and I went to view the father and husband we loved so dearly. I motioned for the rest of my family. This was the man who had been their father for more than twenty-one years and the grandpa the grandchildren had adored. Never again would these little children pound his back, or ride with him on his lawnmower or get rubbed by his whiskers as he'd hold them in his lap. There'd be no more "I'll give you a piece of candy if..." or "Let's ride down on the on the landing and feed the geese and ducks." It was a sad goodbye to Grandpa

The casket was closed. The pallbearers carried his body through the house and out the door. Alvin had left his home forever. We followed and passed between two rows of the American Legion Color Guard from Holmen where Alvin had been a club member. We watched as he was placed in the hearse. Alvin had served as a deputy sheriff for many years and now, to honor him, the funeral procession was led by a patrol car driven by Colin Carrimon, an Indian and member of the La Crosse County Sheriff's Department.

CHAPTER TWENTY-SEVEN

A SIGHT TO BEHOLD

My eyes often gazed out my kitchen window at the hills of Minnesota directly across Lake Onalaska. In February of 1988, two weeks after Alvin died, I turned off the dishwasher to leave the house, when something caught my eye as I glanced out the window.

There, on the top rail of the old red fence in our backyard, was the largest, most beautiful, dark bird I'd ever seen. It was really big, about three feet tall, and its legs were thickly covered with feathers.

I grabbed my small binoculars to see it better and the first thing I noticed were the eyes looking directly at me. I hurried into the bedroom to get the stronger binoculars and study this impressive, dark bird. The way he was perched made it impossible to see the bottom of the tail; the wings were close to his side. His eyes seemed to follow my movement in the house. His breast was a trifle lighter than the rest of his body. The feathers on his legs were so very thick and dark.

I just stood looking and wondered, could it be? Oh God, Alvin, how I miss you. I went to the living room window to view him from the side but he was gone. I wasn't able to see him fly away.

All the bird books point to this having been a young eagle. Impossible. It was too large. Was it a golden eagle? It could have been a rarity. An eagle so close to our home? An eagle facing the house instead of looking out over the frozen lake? An eagle this time of year, before the ice had started to melt?

Or was it a last goodbye from my beloved?

EPILOGUE

The night Alvin died, Wednesday, January 27, 1988, friends and relatives gathered at the home of Richard and Rita Blackdeer for the first meal. Word had spread quickly, for relatives and friends from Baraboo, Wisconsin Dells, Black River Falls, and the La Crosse area had all come to pay homage to him. Many of the foods he loved had been prepared from the time he died to the hour of this first meal.

The next morning, Ralph Mann (the elder of the Bear Clan), Kenny Littlegeorge (his assistant) and other close relatives removed Alvin's belongings from the house. His pictures were turned to the wall. The mirrors were all covered with cloth so there would be no reflections of his spirit.

Thursday and Friday night, large evening meals were shared with more Indians. White people were welcome too. I don't know where they all came from. The meals would start with a prayer, passing the water (the sustainer of life), and the smoking of the peace pipe. Each person present, Indian and white, men, women, and children, all took part in the ceremony.

During these days, our Indian friends and relatives took over my chores of cleaning, cooking, and preparing for the funeral. All the foods Alvin used to love were being prepared for the meal.

A large tarp covered with a tablecloth was placed on our basement floor along with cushions for people to sit on while partaking of the feast. The last meal was held after the burial. Alvin's spirit had been seen by many attending the meals with his friends during those last evenings. They all agreed he was happy and content. This last night was filled with Indian stories, one after another, being told in the Winnebago language. Games were played by young and old, everyone was having a good time.

Then the women who had been preparing the food motioned to the men in charge to set the plates around and put the food on the table cloth. We ate in shifts, there were so many people attending. There was deer meat prepared in stews and different ways Alvin loved. There were chicken and duck dishes. There was muskrat and other wild game. Vegetables of all kinds were in hot dishes and stews. His favorite corn soup and rice and bologna dishes were there. Fry bread was in good supply. Cups of coffee were kept filled as cakes, rolls, cookies, pies and candy pieces were eaten. There was pork crackling soup. Every food Alvin loved during his life was being served at this meal. Each person could eat as much as they wished. Those who were not hungry still took small portions of everything being served.

As the sun rose, Alvin's spirit left us. The blankets, cushions and tablecloth were all removed. Many people got into their cars and left but others were cleaning up, scrubbing floors, changing the furniture around, always with my approval, but all the actual work was done for me. Mirrors were uncovered, Al's picture once more could be shown. All Al's possessions were taken away. After the house was spick-and-span, Rita and others left knowing they had done all they could for me. Only my immediate family remained.

We learned how supportive our Indian family had been. They didn't ask what was to be done; they knew and they all pitched in and did it. They all showed their love and respect for Alvin during those trying days. I will never forget their kindness.

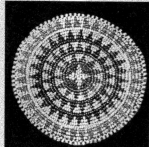

Photo Credits: Marna Holley, Jim Holmlund, *The La Crosse Tribune*, Bennett Studios, David Onsrud, Muriel Blackdeer, the Blackdeer family, Badger history, and Chas Willhoft

1920 Map of Western Wisconsin

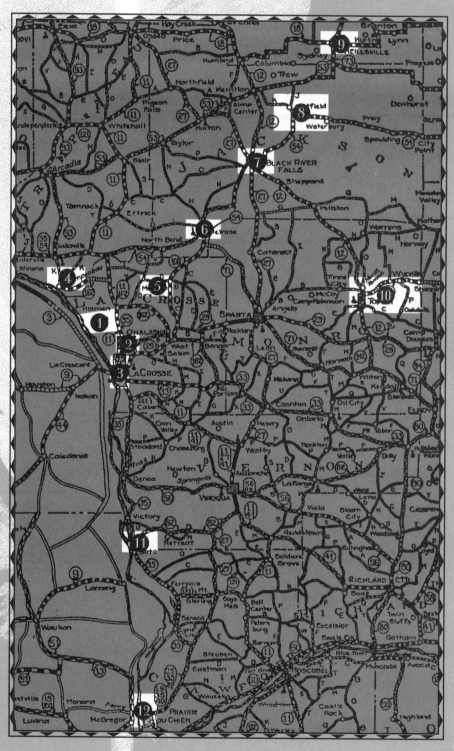

KEY